Father God,

it's me again...Mary

(An imaginative portrayal of the prayer life of Jesus' mother)

By Sharon L. Watson

Copyright © 2012 by Sharon L. Watson

Father God, it's me again...Mary
by Sharon L. Watson

Printed in the United States of America

ISBN 9781619966499

All rights reserved solely by the author. The author guarantees all contents are original and do not infringe upon the legal rights of any other person or work. No part of this book may be reproduced in any form without the permission of the author. The views expressed in this book are not necessarily those of the publisher.

Unless otherwise indicated, Bible quotations are taken from the English Standard Version of the Bible. Copyright © 2001 by Crossway Bibles a publishing ministry of Good News Publishers.

www.xulonpress.com

Lorne,

Thanks for being one of my very best friends! God bless you!

Sharon Watson

Book Dedication

Thank you, Lord, for my mother, the real Ms. June, who not only taught me as one of my Sunday school teachers, but also showed me in her everyday life what it meant to be obedient to her Lord. She was the most gentle, loving woman I ever met and I was truly blessed that you gave me such a mother. I wish to dedicate this book to her memory.

Acknowledgements

I would like to acknowledge and thank many people who were invaluable throughout the process of writing this book:

- To the numerous friends and family who read the unedited version, thank you for your kind words and encouragement.
- To Frank Stirk who edited my book and gave guidance and advice, thank you. Being a writer and editor yourself, I have great respect for your input and expertise in this area. Your belief in this book was a great encouragement.
- To Glen, my best friend, love of my life, my husband, I want to say thank you for nagging me. Your belief in me and this book has kept me pushing myself. You have always been my greatest fan and cheerleader!
- To my Father God, thank you for including me in this project. I truly believe this is ultimately your book, Father, and pray that it bless others as much as it blessed me.

Finally, to my readers, thank you for spending time with this book. My desire is that these pages will glorify our Father God, and that it will touch your lives, drawing you to a closer walk with Him.

Book Reviews

"Though fictional, *Father God, it's me again…Mary*, serves to enliven the senses and creatively engages the reader with real challenges, joys, and struggles. It effectively transports the impact of the story from 1st century Judea to a modern context. Not only does it serve to bridge the distance between the ages, it also helps highlight the real drama of a personal relationship with God and gives the reader a real sense of how the story and that key relationship could have played out in their world. The use of dialogue to bring clarity to the biblical text is novel and yet another example of the author's use of powerful tools to engage the reader's mind. It is a highly enjoyable read that will motivate the reader to engage in an examination of their own faith."

Rev. Douglas McGuire
Pastor-Teacher
Grace Centre for Biblical Studies

"As leader of women's ministries at our church, I see both a need and a desire to have such a book in our library and our homes. Many women want to relate and attempt to understand Mary's prayer journey; this is a unique way to present it. Sharon has shown herself to be a woman of integrity and compassion and these two qualities show in her writing…"

Susan Badke
Women's Ministries Leader

Table of Contents

Prologue xiii

Chapter One – Remembering an Angel's Visit 15

Chapter Two-Joseph's Decision 29

Chapter Three-The Birth 35

Chapter Four – The Shepherds 43

Chapter Five – Simeon's Prophecy 49

Chapter Six-First Steps 55

Chapter Seven – The Magi 59

Chapter Eight-Fleeing to Egypt 66

Chapter Nine-Weeping for the Babies 72

Chapter Ten-Nazareth 76

Chapter Eleven-A Special Friend 79

Chapter Twelve-A Sunset 84

Chapter Thirteen-A Lost Son 89

Chapter Fourteen-Carpentry & Siblings 96

Chapter Fifteen-Joseph Gone 103

Chapter Sixteen-Cousin John 111

Chapter Seventeen-A Wedding in Cana 117

Epilogue 125

Prologue

*I*n the calm of a cooling dusk, peace settled over the hills of Nazareth.

The young Jewish maiden leaned over the wall encompassing the flat rooftop of her home. It was her favorite place to enjoy the quiet after a hectic day. Today was no different as she drew in a deep breath and closed her eyes pondering events of the past few days.

Though considered a woman in society, vestiges of girlhood remained visible in the innocence of warm brown eyes. Those eyes sparkled with youthful hopes and dreams. A wave of dark hair surrounded features shining from an inner beauty born of a gentle, sweet spirit.

Moments before she had watched her father and the neighboring men leave their homes, don prayer shawls, and head towards the synagogue for evening prayers. Smiling, she realized that Joseph would be in that group of faithful worshippers.

The thought of him brought a smile to her face. It was now official – she and Joseph were to wed! Her betrothal continued to fill her mind these days, adding a flush to the healthy glow of her complexion. Her heart leapt with joy each time the realization came to mind.

This was God's answer to her prayers. She had asked for a husband whom she could respect and love. The marriage ceremony was months away, but she knew it would come to pass soon enough. She was promised to him! She felt no fear of her future, only joy, for Joseph was an honorable man. But joy of joys, she also knew, like her, he had a deep love for the Lord.

Her eyes glistened with tears of gratitude and happiness. Raising her face toward a darkening sky, the purity of her voice slowly filled the evening with her favorite psalm of praise. Joy from her overflowing heart spilled into the peace of the dusk, quietly flooding it with her music.

The hush of nature settling for the night intensified as clear notes of adoration wound through the trees. Even birds became silent, paying homage to their Creator. As her song winged its way to heaven, one could picture the angels pausing to bow and worship through the pure notes of her deep love soaring to the Almighty.

> "I will give thanks to You, O Lord, among the peoples;
> I will sing praises to You among the nations.
> For Your steadfast love is great above the heavens;
> Your faithfulness reaches to the clouds.
> Be exalted, O God, above the heavens!
> Let Your glory be over all the earth!"

As the last notes faded, the first evening star came out, sparkling applause in response.

This was her favorite time of day. It was a time she could worship her God. A time she could talk over the day with her heavenly Father. A time she could thank him, or ask for his guidance. It was a time she cherished.

With eyes closed, she allowed the music in her soul to flow through her thoughts into prayer.

Father God, it's me again...Mary.

Chapter One – Remembering the Angel's Visit

"*I* probably should have made two trips," June muttered, juggling an armload of items down the steps leading to the church's Education wing.

"I think I can, I think I can." Puffing anxiously, like the fabled little engine, she shifted her burden to reach for the doorknob of the class.

Balancing her lesson plan, Bible, purse, drinking cups and a plate of cookies, June triumphantly pushed the door open with her hip.

"Success!"

She gloated too soon. The pile of loose papers slipped off the plate of cookies and fanned out across the floor.

"Or maybe not," she sighed.

Putting down her remaining burdens, she leaned over to pick up the scattered pages of today's lesson plan. Her eyes caught the bold headline: 'Life Lessons from Mary'. June remembered how challenged she had felt while preparing the study. Mary's strength of character, her trust and obedience to God, was inspiring.

"Let's try this again," she muttered, finally beginning the routine of setting up for her weekly class.

Working around the room she began raising blinds, cracking the windows open to relieve the stuffiness of a week's stale air. Plumping cushions on the shabby couch and spreading brightly-colored bean bag chairs around in a semi-circle facing the sofa completed her routine. The teen girls in her class seemed to love lounging on the floor.

"Shabby chic-I guess that would describe our décor. More shabby than chic, though," June smiled, surveying the finished arrangement.

Sunday morning. This was her favorite time of the week. With the lights still off, there was a sense of peace in the room. June knew that as soon as she switched on the fluorescent lights a buzz of expectancy would spring the room to attention. It seemed to be preparing for the vibrant energy that would flow in as the group of 13-to 15-year-old girls bounced through the door. Then the room would reverberate with giggles and laughter. But for now, in the dim light of semi-darkness, it still spoke of the calmness and peace June loved.

Why have I agreed to take this class? She wondered again.

This had to be one of the noisiest classes and it was certainly one of the hardest groups to keep interested or focused on topic, that's for sure. Facing these girls always gave her a nervous stomach.

Why did I have to eat that extra muffin for breakfast, she moaned?

Satisfied that the room was set up in an inviting array, she brought out the plate of homemade chocolate chip cookies. At least she could stop some of the giggling and get a word in while they were busy munching on goodies. Who said bribery doesn't work? A jug of cold water and glasses were set beside the cookies on the small coffee table placed as the centre hub of the circle.

Humming under her breath, June quietly sang, "This is the day the Lord has made. We will rejoice and be glad in it."

Her spirit lifted with the lilting song. She decided it wasn't that bad teaching the teenage girls' Sunday morning class. They were nice girls, even if it felt like she had run a mental marathon by the end of class.

As giggles were heard floating down the hall, June could tell that Mandy and Lauren were the first ones arriving.

"So it begins."

She took a deep breath and turned on the lights.

The first two arrivals shattered the peace of the classroom as they burst through the doorway vying for June's attention.

"Morning, Ms. June," they chorused, followed immediately by tales from their week being relayed simultaneously.

Mandy and Lauren were inseparable friends. June smiled at the two carbon-copy girls as they chattered and gesticulated with their usual enthusiasm. As always they were similar in dress and appearance, so that they looked like twins.

"Just the bestest of best friends!" was their typical reply when this similarity was mentioned.

More often than not, they would talk in a duet of words, jumping back and forth between each girl, volleying as one took up the story mid-sentence from the other, and back again. It was an uncanny knack they had, and tended to make June's head swim and neck ache from trying to bounce back and forth between the two.

"Good morning, Mandy. Good morning, Lauren."

She interrupted their barrage of words, pointing them towards the circle.

"You're first, so choose your favorite seats."

"I get the red bean bag!" Lauren squealed, leaping past Mandy to claim her favorite spot.

"That's okay by me. I want the sofa today."

Mandy curled into the corner armrest, punching the pillows around her until she looked like a baby chick in a cozy nest.

Both girls eyed the cookies, sneaking peeks at June to see if they could snatch one unseen before the rest of the class assembled.

Without glancing their way, June intoned, "Leave the cookies alone. Not until everyone's here. You know the rules!"

She knew these two would always push the limits just to see if they could bend the rules their way.

At the sound of stomping feet running down the hallway stairs, June knew there were more girls on the way. *Graceful they are not*, she smiled to herself, as three new arrivals crowded through the door, tripping over each other, trying to be first to lay claim to their favorite seats.

June gave Tina a special welcoming smile. At 16, Tina was the oldest and should have moved on to the older youth class, but because of some learning disorders she fit better with the younger teen girls. Luckily they all seemed to accept her, though she tended to be the one left out when the others paired off.

Rebecca and Marie completed the small class of five girls. Watching the last three girls stumble and trip over bean bags, knocking into the coffee table, finally getting themselves settled, June once again counted her blessings that it was a small class.

I don't think the furniture, or my nerves, could take any more noise and activity, she thought.

"Good morning, ladies." As always they giggled when she called them 'ladies'. "I hope you had a wonderful week."

A cacophonous burst of five voices began to share events from their week. In mock horror, June held up hands as if fending off the sudden attack of voices. The noise gradually receded to laughter and chuckles as they watched Ms. June try to hide from their onslaught.

Finally the girls settled to wait their turns. One thing they loved about Ms. June was that she always encouraged everyone to share their thoughts, so they would all be heard eventually.

"I want each of us to begin a habit today-a habit that I'm sure was an important part in the life of the woman we are studying today. This is a habit we need to practice each day of the week, not just on Sundays. I'm talking about the habit of prayer. We can talk to God anywhere and at anytime, so let's start now."

June bowed her head, waiting a moment as the rustle of nervous bodies quieted.

"Dear Father, we praise you for the blessing of this day. Thank you for your church, and the opportunity to worship and learn about you through your Word, the Bible. I want to thank you for the blessing of this class and the privilege of teaching and learning with these girls. Help us to learn to seek you and love you more each day. Amen."

With sighs, the girls shuffled into comfortable positions once again.

"Go ahead and help yourselves to the cookies," June offered.

The descent of eager hands upon the plate threatened a capsizing, but miraculously it remained flat on the table, wobbling as it settled from the attack. Shaking her head, June marveled that these girls seemed to eat constantly yet never gained an ounce.

Taking the opportunity of semi-silence while mouths were full of crumbs, June took a deep breath and plunged into the lesson for this week.

"Today we're looking at the life of Mary, the mother of Jesus."

A few groans could be heard at the topic. She recognized those moans, just like storm cloud warnings. There was a definite threat that the dreaded glaze of boredom would descend upon the group if she didn't catch their interest immediately.

June continued doggedly, "What do you know about Mary?

Anyone with a fairly empty mouth can answer."

Giggling, Mandy and Lauren quickly stuffed another bite into their mouths. They knew this would effectively prevent them from having to reply.

"Mary was Jesus' mother. She was also perfect. What more is there to know?"

Marie always brought questions down to their simplest form. After years of attending Sunday school she seemed to feel she had heard all of the answers and now just wanted to get the Bible learning over with as soon as possible.

"You're right and you're wrong, Marie."

June smiled at the look of surprise widening Marie's eyes. She was definitely not used to being wrong about anything.

"Yes, Mary was Jesus' mother, but she was not perfect. Mary was human, with normal human emotions, worries, hopes, dreams and fears. The Bible tells us in Romans 3:23, 'all have sinned.' So we know Mary was not perfect, just as no one is, or ever was. No one, that is, except Jesus himself."

Finally she had the focus of five pairs of eyes. Five mouths had stopped munching, a few frozen in mid-bite, as the thought of Mary not being perfect hit them.

"Did you know that Mary was a teenager, probably about your age, when she received the angel's message, telling her she would bear the son of God?"

"No way!" Lauren gasped.

"Yes way! In those days girls got engaged when they came of childbearing age. So she was probably about 14 years old when she became engaged to Joseph. Just imagine the concerns or worries that must have gone through her mind after the angel left. How overwhelmed and alone she may have felt, suddenly facing unknown consequences of what was about to happen to her."

"What do you mean?" Mandy asked, licking a chocolate smudge off her finger.

"Well, just think about it! Mary is engaged, not married-but she's going to have a baby. You can't hide something like that! So how do you tell your parents and your fiancé that you've seen an angel who told you you're going to bear God's Son?"

Marie looked smug as she answered, "Why tell them anything at all? She could simply wait until after she's married. Then she says the baby is her husband's and was born early. That's what my neighbor's daughter did."

June shook her head sadly at the solution Maria had offered.

"Unfortunately, that wouldn't work in this case. First, that would be a dishonest approach, and I can't imagine Mary choosing to be dishonest. But you should realize that it may have been several months or possibly more than a year before her marriage was to take place. Engagements tended to last a year or two. As you can imagine, it would be a little hard to hide the fact that you have a baby in your arms under the wedding canopy!"

"So what did she do?" Tina looked concerned as she struggled with the problem.

"The Bible doesn't tell us exactly what happened, but we can guess that Mary told her parents and Joseph. In the gospel of Matthew, it says Joseph had a difficult decision to make. Should he marry someone who is pregnant, not by him, and who is telling a most improbable tale of bearing the Son of God? Or, should he quietly break their engagement? Mary would then have to live apart from society.

"Thankfully, in that day they rarely stoned people for adultery any more. It was a law that would have been carried out in Moses' time, centuries before, and it still could have been enforced in Mary's time.

But even if her life was not threatened, the divorce or dissolving of her engagement to Joseph would leave Mary branded as a sinful, fallen woman."

"But that's not fair! Why didn't people believe her?" Rebecca burst out.

"Would you? How fantastic and unbelievable the truth must have seemed. Even those who knew Mary well would probably think she was covering up a sinful act. How many of us embellish the truth when we're in trouble and want to deny, or hide, our guilt?

"But Mary, although not perfect, must have been a young woman of strong character who had a deep devotion to God. She obviously loved and trusted God. She was obedient even though it would complicate her life. God had chosen her to be the Savior's mother. What an awesome honor, but what an awkward truth to tell! Even so, she was honest with those who needed to know what was happening, even in the face of what it could mean for her future. It could have meant she would lose the marriage she had been promised."

"So why didn't God take care of everything? He was responsible! He should have made everything right!"

Marie's eyes flashed at the thought of the injustices Mary would suffer for her obedience.

June smiled at the passion in the young faces around her.

"He did, Marie! You'll see how well God took care of everything. Not only at this time in Mary's life, but over the years as well.

"You might remember when the angel appeared to Mary, he also told her about a miracle happening to Elizabeth, Mary's cousin. Elisabeth was much older than Mary, more like an aunt in age. She hadn't been able to have children her whole married life but now she was expecting a child. Her son was promised to be the one who was to come before the Messiah, declaring the way of the Lord!

"So you see God provided a place for Mary to go. She lived for three months with her cousin. It was Elizabeth who first believed in Mary's miraculous pregnancy. Maybe it was easier for her to believe because of her own miraculous pregnancy. In these surroundings, Mary must have felt accepted and encouraged as she waited to hear Joseph's decision."

* * * * *

O Lord, how glorious you are above the earth! My soul will sing your praise forever, as I rejoice in you, my God and my Savior!

Father God, I can't help but praise you, as I prepare to sleep. Lying in the open under your glorious sky, I marvel at the beauty the night has brought with it. I could gaze forever at the exquisite night sky you've created. The stars dazzle, brightly dancing and shimmering, forming a diamond carpet for your feet.

This is my favorite time of day. Although I crave the solitude of Elizabeth's rooftop, where I've laid my sleeping pallet, still I know I'm never alone. Your cool caress is in the gentle breeze, and the fragrance of night blooms wash me with your peace, covering my soul with a sweet calm. It's so still. I feel I'm alone with you, Lord.

It's hard to believe I'm not dreaming these days. I've lost track of how many times I've thought, "Surely I'll wake soon and everything will be back to normal". Yet I know my life will never be normal again. Everything has been turned upside down.

I can close my eyes and remember the brilliant image of your angel as he appeared before me. His presence was radiant, a light more dazzling than the sun, yet not blinding in its purity. Falling to my knees, I was sure I must be dead. My heart thundered, pulsing so loudly in my ears the angel's voice sounded like I was listening underwater. His words seemed distant and I couldn't grasp their meaning at first. Now I can't get Gabriel's words out of my mind. All day long, as a cool and refreshing stream, they run over and over in my mind.

'Favored one,' Gabriel called me.

Joy fills my heart! To know I've found favor with you, Lord! A constant bubbling well of happiness wants to burst out in laughter and praise.

I've talked to you, Father, from my earliest memories on, but now I know how personal a God you are. Though a simple, lowly handmaid, you know me and call me by name, 'Mary.' I've always known you were there. In many ways I felt and saw your presence in the world around me, but I never expected to receive a personal and miraculous announcement from you.

Lord, I confess I was hesitant when the angel proclaimed I was chosen to bear your Son. I felt confused and, though I don't remember doing so, I must have uttered my question out loud.

'How will this be, since I am a virgin?'

Gabriel's reply calmed my fears. His answer is burned like a banner across my mind.

"The Holy Spirit will come upon you, and the power of the Most High will overshadow you; therefore the child to be born will be called holy—the Son of God."

The Son of God!

I don't think I know how to be the mother of God's Son. I know you are all-wise, but I don't feel worthy. Still, I trust you, Lord. I depend on your strength because I know, by myself, I'm weak.

Yesterday I saw a shadow which pronounced the growing curve of my stomach. I couldn't help smiling at the mystery, for I know hidden within is the growing form of God's Son! I don't understand how the miracle happened to me, but I'm so happy that you chose me! I always dreamt of one day having children, especially since my engagement to my beloved Joseph.

Joseph! O Lord, you know this news weighs heavy on his heart. I'll never forget when I told him what happened. I was sure he'd believe me, yet I watched him slump from the pain and shock of disbelief. Suddenly my heart too felt a burden, knowing what this could mean for our future. My joyous announcement had become a weight to Joseph, a burden despised like the packs the Roman soldiers force us to carry.

I know he's concerned for my safety, being unmarried and pregnant. I'm sure he wants to believe me, yet he can't accept that your Holy Spirit has brought this child into being. I don't blame him, for it's not everyday such miracles happen.

Father, give Joseph a peace about your child. I don't know what he'll decide to do. I'm afraid he may choose to put me aside. Yet it's a decision he alone can make. I knew he didn't need me around, clouding his emotions, so I had to leave Nazareth. Father, I know that you'll care for me and this child of ours-but I still miss Joseph. My heart mourns over the hurt and disappointment he's feeling. No one seems able to believe in this miracle, except my cousin Elizabeth.

I rejoiced when Gabriel told me of Elizabeth's blessing. After the response from Joseph and my family, I didn't know what to do. Then it hit me. I can go to Elizabeth! I'll help her as she is heavy with child and getting on in age as well. Surely she, if anyone, will understand my condition and believe the miracle you are bringing about.

There was relief in the face of my family as I packed for the trip. They tried to hide their feelings from me. Still I could tell that I'd become an embarrassment to them. Falling from beloved daughter

Father God, it's me again...Mary

to someone they don't want around is hard to bear. It's obvious they doubt my honesty, my purity, and possibly my sanity. I needed to get away from the stares, the furtive whispers that always seemed to follow me. It had become more than I could bear.

I knew eventually when my marriage took place I'd leave the home of my childhood to start a family of my own. Many times I'd dreamt how that day would be. There'd be some sorrow at leaving my parents and my sweet sister, but it would be overshadowed by the joy and excitement of a wedding and knowing I was beginning a new life with Joseph.

Instead I'm haunted by a memory of hugs filled with tears of sorrow, not joy. As I walked out the doorway of my home, I turned to wave goodbye and nearly wept at the clouded eyes of those I love. Instead of joy in their gaze, I saw hurt, disappointment, and sadness. I realized I was indeed leaving home for good, beginning a new life, though not as the young bride I'd imagined.

O Lord, you were so gracious when you led me to my kinswoman's home. It's become a haven of rest and encouragement. Lying here, on Elizabeth and Zechariah's rooftop, I feel your protection surrounding me in the stillness of the night. Thank you, Father God, for your watchful care of me and this child I carry. I'm surer than ever that no matter what happens you will be our Protector.

I'll never forget the welcome I received arriving at the front door of Elizabeth's home. What a shock as her first words of greeting were praises for the special child I'm bearing! Her cry of joy and welcome is engraved in my mind.

"Blessed are you among women, and blessed is the fruit of your womb!"

I hadn't even told her yet! I felt reassurance through the revelation you gave Elizabeth. Lord, you knew it was just what I needed to hear.

What a difference! Her joyous praise, compared to the denials from those I'd left behind. Elizabeth's words helped me to drop the burden I'd carried from home. Once again I realized I am indeed 'blessed among women'.

While I'm gone from home, Lord, please watch over my family and dear Joseph. Help him make the right decision. He must wholeheartedly believe this child is yours, or I can't marry him. Any doubt would become a wall between us. He'd never be able to trust me fully, or love this Son of ours completely, as I already do.

O Lord, I'm going to have a child! Our Messiah is finally coming! The thought is amazing, exciting, frightening and awe-inspiring all at the same time. I keep jumping from emotion to emotion. One minute I'm singing songs of praise to you and the next, crying, as I remember saying farewell, leaving my home.

Our people have waited so long for the miracle of the Messiah, yet no one seems to believe that he could come in our time. At long last the 'Promised One' is coming-here, now, and to me, your lowly handmaid! I don't blame them for doubting. It is truly a miraculous and strange tale.

This morning I woke again feeling like I was living in a dream. Reality hit as quick as the familiar wave of nausea when I arose from my bed. Everyday I see and feel changes happening in my body. What a glorious thought! A Son – your holy child is being knit together in my womb!

"He will be great and will be called the Son of the Most High."

Gabriel's words keep repeating in my mind at the oddest times of the day. While I'm helping with the wash, or carrying water from the well, suddenly I hear the echo of his voice whisper the truth in my mind and my heart pounds, excited and joyful. But today was the most wonderful! O Lord-for the first time I felt the fluttering movement of our child. The angel's words reverberated in my soul, like crashing waves of a gong, proclaiming once again, 'He will be great, and will be called the Son of the Most High.'!

Father God, I feel wrapped in the comfort of your presence, drowsy and content, ready to sleep. I can't resist one last look at the star-studded sky as I marvel at some of the grandest creations you have made, Lord. Yet, I'm in awe, for I realize, of all your creations, the greatest is happening now, within me, in the tiny form of the child I bear.

Thank you, Lord. You bent down to earth and touched this heart, soul and body of mine. You honored me, including me in your plan to bring peace and salvation to your people.

I am your handmaid, Father. May I ever be your faithful servant.

Chapter Two – Joseph's Decision

"Ms. June, please tell us. What happened to Mary?"

Tina's anxious tone was heart-wrenching in its innocence.

"We know what happened, Tina! Obviously Joseph married her. Remember all the Christmas plays we've done!"

Maria looked with amazement at Tina, annoyed that she could be silly enough not to realize the connection between the Bethlehem birth and this Mary they studied today.

June glanced at Tina and gave her an appreciative smile. She seemed to have grasped the desperate situation Mary had truly faced.

"You know, Maria, though we can look back and know things turned out fine for Mary, you should try to realize Mary didn't know what was going to happen. Be like Tina and forget all that you know for now. Put yourself into Mary's time and place. Feel the uncertainty of her future. Her life had just taken a 180 degree about-face."

Tina still looked to be on the edge of her seat.

June continued, "Well, it almost didn't happen the way we know now. Joseph had made his decision all right…"

"Like Maria said," Rebecca interrupted, "he obviously decided to go ahead and marry her, or our Christmas celebrations would not include Joseph in the story."

June continued, ignoring the interruption. "Joseph's decision was to quietly divorce Mary."

"No!" Tina's eyes started to glisten at the thought of the loss Mary faced. She has such a sensitive heart, June realized, and carried on quickly.

"Don't worry-once again God intervened. After Joseph had struggled and made this difficult choice, he fell asleep, probably emotionally exhausted. His life was in turmoil.

"God stepped in as the Great Provider. He sent his angel to give direction to Joseph. Again God's plans were announced, this time to Joseph. Did you realize that just as God chose Mary, so he also chose Joseph? He knew Mary and her baby would need a strong husband and father to protect and provide for them.

"We're told that Joseph awoke from the vision of his angelic visitor and immediately obeyed God's instructions. He went to bring Mary home to be his wife."

At that pronouncement, Tina relaxed back into her bean bag chair, a satisfied smile on her face. June smiled as she noticed the other girls also sigh with contentment. It seems these teens were not quite as nonchalant about Mary's plight as they would have her believe. Everyone seemed to be getting caught up in the idea of Mary's predicament.

"We can only imagine the relief Mary must have felt when Joseph came to bring her home, and the joy she felt knowing God had also given Joseph a personal message about the baby. It was a Jewish tradition for the father to name the new baby. By revealing to Joseph the name chosen for his Son, it would seem God the Heavenly Father was passing that privilege on to Joseph, the man who would be his earthly father. And we all know the name of the baby was to be Jesus."

* * * * *

He's come for me! I can hardly believe it, Lord. You've answered my prayers in a marvelous way. Even beyond what I could imagine.

I scarcely dared believe it was true when Elizabeth called me in from the garden.

"Mary, come quick. Joseph is here to take you home!"

My heart leapt with joy. The weeds were forgotten as I jumped to my feet and raced to the house. There he stood in the main room, waiting for me. Such a look of tender love and joy shone from his eyes and I knew immediately he no longer had doubts about this baby I feel growing within me.

Without a word, Joseph took my hand and led me back outside into the garden where he shared the vision he had received from you, Lord. He said the decision to put me aside, to obtain a divorce from our engagement, was one he dreaded but I understood that as an honorable man he felt it was the only path open to him. It was with a heavy heart that he finally fell asleep, exhausted and drained from the struggle of making this choice, when your messenger once again appeared. Joseph was as amazed to hear the same message as I. Your angel brought the magnificent proclamation of your Son's coming, but this time to my beloved Joseph.

"Do not fear to take Mary as your wife; for that which is conceived in her is from the Holy Spirit. She will bear a son, and you shall call his name Jesus, for he will save his people from their sins."

He will save our people from their sins! What a mysterious message. Neither Joseph nor I understand completely what this means but we have chosen to trust in you, Father.

We stood in the garden while he told me of the angel's visit. O

Father, his love warmed my heart just like your sun was warming my head. I was almost afraid to look away from that beloved face. This answer to prayer was one that I had often seen in my dreams. Now there he stood, solid and real, your heavenly rays glistening on his dark curls. My eyes filled with tears of joy, even as his beloved face grew serious. Taking both my hands, he faced me.

"Will you forgive me?"

I shook my head, trying to tell him he needn't say anymore, but he carried on.

"I didn't believe you. I didn't trust that you were telling me the truth. I wondered how I could believe such a crazy tale."

He smiled, and gently caressed back the hair blowing across my face, placing it behind my ear.

"But if your story is crazy, then so is mine, for I too have seen the Lord's angel. If you will still have me, I wish to fulfill our engagement agreement. I've dreamed a long time that I would hear you call me your husband. It would be my honor to provide and protect and love you and this Son you shall bear."

I could contain my joy no longer. Throwing my arms around him, I gripped him tightly in a hug of joy and gratitude. A few tears of happiness dampened his tunic and muffled my cry of acceptance.

"Yes, yes, dear Joseph! I too have waited a long time and would be proud to be your wife."

His strong carpenter's arms returned my hug with incredible gentleness, as though holding a precious alabaster jar, fearing it could shatter.

His voice was muffled against my hair, as he whispered gently, "Jesus will be known as our Son. But we will not know one another as husband and wife in truth until after this child has been born.

He'll be born in purity. We will cherish and raise him as best we can, with God's help."

Lord, what a wise, loving man you chose to be my husband and to be a father to your Son. Thank you for the blessing of Joseph.

Elizabeth and Zechariah celebrated our reunion last evening. It struck me at one point, during our laughter and the joy, that this may be as close as we get to a wedding celebration meal. Considering the circumstances, our marriage will take place in a much quieter setting, with little fanfare and celebration. But Lord, it was such a joyous evening I know I couldn't have enjoyed any celebration more. We spoke of the miracles of these two expected babies, marveling at what you are doing and rejoicing in the honor of serving you.

While I'm excited to be going, I'm still sad to be leaving Elizabeth at this time. Since Zechariah was struck deaf and dumb during her months of her pregnancy, she's appreciated having me here to help her and talk with her. She's been such an encouragement to me too! In only a short time she'll be delivered of this miracle son that was promised them. Nonetheless she's insisting I return at once with Joseph. Though he'd be willing to wait a while, Elizabeth is wise and knows he shouldn't take much time away from his livelihood in the carpentry shop. Even more so now that he has a family to provide for and take care of. Father, be with Elizabeth as her time draws near. Protect her and deliver her son safely.

My hands are shaking so much with excitement it's hard to fold my clothes and pack my bag. I'm going home! I'm going home to become the wife of Joseph, in name if not in fact at this time. That time will come for us, but for now I praise you, Lord. You've once again answered my prayers and provided for us.

It will be a bittersweet homecoming. Rumors and gossip will probably surround us, but now that Joseph knows the truth and believes in me, I know we can stand against any whispers and frowns thrown our way. Others may raise eyebrows and be critical, saying this baby was conceived in dishonor before we were properly wed, but Joseph and I know the truth. This child was miraculously conceived and is a great honor from you, Lord.

Again I must say another goodbye, take another journey and face a new beginning in my life. Only you know the paths my life will follow, Lord. I give this one to you and thank you because I know you'll guard our footsteps, guiding us as we travel this road together.

I have a new family – Joseph, your unborn Son and you, Lord. As always, you are our Heavenly Father.

Chapter Three – The Birth

"So Joseph took Mary back home to Nazareth," June continued the story.

"Wait a minute," Lauren broke in, talking around her latest chocolate chip cookie, "I thought Jesus was born in Bethlehem."

"Yeah, that's right!" Mandy exclaimed, sitting up in her comfy nest of pillows, surrounding her on the couch. "So how'd that happen?" She reached over to the dwindling plate of cookies and grabbed another to pop into her mouth.

Maria rolled her eyes and sighed. "Don't you guys remember anything from your Sunday School classes? It was the census!"

"The 'what-sus'?" Mandy mumbled while trying to keep from spraying cookie crumbs everywhere.

"Only talk with empty mouths, please," came June's casual reminder. "Can you explain a little more about what the census was, Maria?"

"It was a decree that came from the government. They wanted an accurate counting of the population so they could tax them."

"That's a good explanation. The census would be used probably for taxing and maybe for other purposes. They might have wanted to know how many men were of fighting age, for instance. Anyway, whatever the purpose, the decree came that the men were to register themselves and their families, at the town of their ancestry. Why do you suppose Joseph and Mary had to travel to Bethlehem?"

"Because that's where Jesus was to be born?"

Tina tentatively threw out the guess, blushing as snickers burst from the other girls.

June ignored the giggles and took Tina's answer seriously, nodding her head thoughtfully.

"You've made a very good point, Tina. God had indeed foretold that the birthplace of the Messiah would be Bethlehem, so we know it was in God's plan that Mary and Joseph travel there before Jesus' birth. But that wasn't foremost in their minds when they left on this trip.

"Though Joseph and Mary's hometown was Nazareth, Joseph was from the family line of King David, and Bethlehem was known as the 'City of David.' So Bethlehem was where Joseph was required to register his family for the census."

Glancing around the circle of girls, June could see an argument building in Rebecca's pursed lips. Sure enough, crossing her arms in defiance, Rebecca burst out her question.

"So if God is the 'Great Provider' as you put it, why didn't he have a better place for Jesus to be born? I mean a stable is not my idea of a great birthing room!"

"First of all, do you know what stables were like at that time, in that country?" June queried, trying to defuse the moment.

"Sort of like a wooden lean-to…"

"Or small barn-like building…"

"Filled with animals, hay and feeding toughs…"

"And probably very noisy…"

"And it probably stank, too!"

June's eyes bounced between Mandy and Lauren as their answers ricocheted back and forth. Shaking her head slightly to stop the dizzying effect these two had when they really got going, June smiled in answer.

"I know you've all seen nativity scenes, showing a wooden structure and a wooden manger, used for a cradle. You may be surprised to know that the animals were stabled in natural caves found in the hillsides surrounding the towns. Wooden structures were not common in that country. The manger, or feeding trough, was often natural stone shelves, carved or hollowed out to hold the animal feed. But you're correct in saying there would have been lots of animals, and noise and all the smells associated with a stable."

"So why didn't God provide something better?" Maria queried, taking up a similar posture as Rebecca.

"I want you to stop and think for a minute," June paused to look each girl in the eyes, making sure she had their attention. "Where would you rather give birth? Amongst a crowd of strangers, crammed together in a courtyard? Don't forget, the town of Bethlehem was overcrowded because of the census and there would have been little privacy. They were sardined into an area not meant for such an inflated population. Or would you rather have your first baby in the presence of uninterested animals?

"God provided Mary a place that was away from busy streets, away from the crowds and all the noise and smells they brought with them. Instead she shared a space filled with a different kind of noise and smell, but also filled with warmth from the animals housed in the stable. In these surroundings she could give birth in relative privacy, away from the curious ears and eyes of strangers, during the pain of childbirth."

Father God, it's me again...Mary

* * * * *

I don't know what to do Lord. Pain like I've never imagined keeps streaking through me. I'm trying not to let Joseph see how much it hurts. He's anxious enough already. This child of yours may be born here on the road if we don't find shelter soon.

My back's on fire. Walking is impossible, yet each step of this donkey I'm riding sends lightning striking across my belly and up my back. An occasional gasp manages to burst from my lips, though I try to stifle them. Joseph keeps turning anxious eyes towards me, stopping our progress to check on me. O Lord, it doesn't matter if we're moving or standing still, I'm in agony and need to lie down soon.

All the other travelers on their way to Bethlehem have long since overtaken and passed us. We're the only ones left on the darkening road. I can tell Joseph is getting nervous about traveling alone especially since night will fall soon, but he tries to hide his worry from me. He needn't be concerned. I can't seem to focus on anything right now except holding my seat on the donkey through each seizure as knifing pain shoots through every nerve in my body. We must be close to Bethlehem as I can see a few lights up ahead. I smile weakly at my husband, trying to wipe some of the worry lines off his face.

"Please don't stop. I'm fine. We must carry on, Joseph. We'll be in Bethlehem soon."

My sudden gasp, as I double over the donkey's back doesn't help ease his fears, though. Lord, help me stop crying out in anguish. We need shelter soon. I don't want to give birth to your Son at the side of a dirty road.

The relief I felt as we passed the first homes entering Bethlehem is wearing off. The streets are so crowded, even in the growing dusk we can tell how swollen the population has become because of the government's census decree.

Already Joseph has asked dozens of people for directions to an inn, or a private dwelling home where we can rent shelter.

"No room anywhere" is repeated over and over.

Shaking heads, curious eyes stare at me, as I grip the rope with white knuckles, my breath rasping out in pain. Joseph is pointed the way to an inn, but people shake their heads hopelessly at our quest. I feel the stares, some sympathetic, some just curious, watching us shuffle off in the inn's direction.

Everyone says there's no room anywhere, Lord. What are we to do? This is your child, Father. Please provide for us once again.

The innkeeper is harassed because of the crowds. He's speaking so abruptly to my dear Joseph. Still I hear Joseph plead with him for some space. He turns towards me, a hopeless look in his eyes. Joseph must see the anguish I'm trying to contain, for he redoubles his efforts with the innkeeper. There's desperation in his shaking voice.

"Give us anything, please! All we need is a corner, a small nook, somewhere out of the public roadway, where my wife can give birth."

As he continues to implore the innkeeper for space, I feel another spasm gripping me. O God, please help me!

It must be the innkeeper's wife I hear in the background. Though the innkeeper shakes his head, he finally gives us an option. The stable! What a place to have your Son delivered into this world, Father! I can't bring myself to protest, I only know I need to get off the torturous back of this donkey and rest. A bed of hay in the animal's cave will be a luxury right now. It'll be private, if nothing else.

Thankfully the stable is not far behind the main town, a cave formed in the hillside. Thank you, Lord, you've brought us to a haven, away from prying eyes. The surroundings are dark and have the added blessing of solitude, which I crave right now.

Joseph lifts me from the donkey's back. My feet are numb from riding and I'm grateful for his gentle care as he lowers me onto the straw spread out to cushion the hard earthen floor. The musty odors of animals and hay overwhelm me at first, but I'm grateful because I'm no longer suffering the jostling motion of riding.

The relief of lying back against the straw is short-lived. Another contraction crashes over me, taking my breath away, causing a sharp cry from its impact. Dear God, I don't know how much I can stand, or how much strength I have left. I'm worn out from the journey of the last several days. Help me!

The innkeeper's wife has sent her servant girl. Thank you, Lord! She has brought in an extra lamp, and a basin of clean water.

Joseph is trying to help me, cooling my forehead, wiping sweat caused by pain, from my brow. I pray that soon I'll be delivered from these labor pains, and this little one will push his way into the world.

Another wave is building inside. I desperately want to focus on you, Lord. Let my body relax through the pain. I don't want to fight it! Help me allow the door to his world to open, so we can welcome him into our arms and our hearts. My energy is ebbing as each wave and contraction builds in strength and duration.

Lord, I'm so thankful for Joseph! He's been my strength. Sitting behind me, I can lean back against his strong chest, and listen to his heart beating strong and sure. He's so gentle, holding my hands, whispering words of comfort and encouragement. I even hear him whispering a prayer to you, Lord. This baby so long awaited seems to be taking so long to arrive.

Suddenly waves no longer crash, tearing at me. I can feel a new sensation tugging at me. This little one is ready to push his way out. I must help him. Tightly I squeeze the hands holding mine and groan as the new pain builds. A sense of urgency and excitement energizes me. Determined to help my Son push his way into a new existence, I give my last burst of strength to him.

It is done! He is here. Your baby is finally nestled on the cloth laid down to receive him. My lifeline to him is cut and gently Joseph cleans the Son who has changed our lives forever.

As Joseph places him in my arms, I'm flooded with tenderness and joy. Finally I can gaze at my perfect Son. His little face is beautiful-red, wet and wrinkled in cries of shock-but so beautiful nonetheless. I'm a mother! This fragile baby depends on me for his every need. O Lord, what a privilege, and what an awesome task you've given us.

Gently I wrap him tightly in the clean cloths saved especially for his swaddling. Joseph places fresh hay in the stone manger carved in the rock beside us, covering it with a soft blanket for our baby to sleep on. As I hold this precious little form nestled against my breast he instinctively turns seeking my warmth and nourishment with a sigh of contentment. After the bed is prepared for our little one, Joseph joins me, smiling at the picture we must make. A mother and child cuddling together on a delivery bed made of straw.

"His name is Jesus," Joseph pronounces with awe and wonder. Gently he caresses the small head covered with dark, downy hair.

"He will be great and will be called the Son of the Most High," I reply, reverently repeating the angel's words proclaimed so many months ago.

Here he is at last, Father, your Son, Jesus. Thank you, Lord. It was you who provided the place and watched over his birth.

Now exhausted from the labor of delivery, both Jesus and I are ready to sleep. His eyes are already closed and quietly Joseph reaches for him, placing him on the soft bed he has made.

"You must rest, Mary. You need to build up your strength now."

He helps me onto a clean pallet, cushioned by straw on the hard cave floor. With one last contented look at my sleeping Son, the fog of tiredness seeks to overtake me.

Yet, Lord, there is one more lucid thought forming before I slip into a weary sleep. I realize that you, our Heavenly Father, are here in the form of your Son. The Son of God, so tiny and helpless, is lying enthroned within an earthen cave carved by your hand, cradled on a rock you formed to support your sleeping Son. I realize now these surroundings that seemed too humble are suitable, for you made them. What hands could form so precious a birthplace to contain the treasure of your Son? None but the hands of the Creator of the heavens and earth!

I can almost hear the celebration in heaven as I lie here drifting into an exhausted rest. Yet no noise of rejoicing crowds surrounds us. Only a breeze whispers across the hillside, music from animals crowding the cave, fill it with their warmth and the lulling song of their nighttime rustling and lowing. It's the peace of your presence filling this holy place that follows me into my dreams as I drift to sleep.

Thank you, Father. Your Son is wonderfully and marvelously made.

Chapter Four – The Shepherds

"Ms. June," Tina paused, hesitating to continue with her question.

Glancing at Rebecca, Tina blushed as she spied the rolling of eyes she and Maria shared over what they presumed was going to be another stupid question.

"What is it, Tina?" June prompted.

She'd also caught the interaction of the two girls, and wanted to encourage a nervous Tina to bring all of her questions before the group.

"Please don't hesitate to ask any question you want."

"Well, it's just that all the Nativity scenes have so many people in them. You said when Jesus was born there was only Mary, Joseph and baby Jesus. Where did all of the others come from?"

"You're right, Tina. Others did arrive that night. They were given a special invitation to join in the celebration of Jesus' birth. Anyone remember who those greatly honored people were?"

"The shepherds!" Mandy and Lauren chorused together, followed by giggles.

"That's right. God sent his angel to announce his Son's birth to shepherds followed by a whole choir of angels to celebrate with them. Just imagine! God sent this heavenly invitation to none other than a small handful of simple shepherds. These men spent their lives on the outskirts of the Jewish religious community because their livelihood often made them religiously 'unclean' and unable to participate in many of the religious ceremonies."

"How could they treat them like that? I mean, their own King David from the Old Testament, started out as a shepherd!"

June smiled at Rebecca's question. It seemed ironic that Rebecca, so astonished at prejudices from eras past, was blind to her own prejudices. She could judge someone like Tina as less worthy or less acceptable, but couldn't see the obvious connection.

"These were simple men who spent many nights on the hillside with their flocks, especially during lambing season. They were there to help if problems arose, and to protect the young ones from predators. The Jewish laws carried many rules about ritual washing, which would have been impossible for these shepherds to observe while living outside."

"But why would that make them unclean?" Maria queried.

"The Jewish religion had hundreds of rules and regulations that the people had to observe, many of them in order to be considered 'clean'. The ritual washings are just one example. They would also have been considered unclean whenever they had to touch a dead lamb.

"But Jesus' birth was announced first to the shepherds. Maybe God was showing how he valued all people, no matter their skill or station in life."

Tina's eyes lit up as she suddenly discovered a special truth. "So the shepherds were considered less worthy by many people, but God considered them special and told them first." With clasped hands, eyes sparkling, she exclaimed, "Imagine getting an angelic invitation to Jesus' birthday party!"

"What a great way to put it!" June grinned.

A ripple of excitement flowed amongst the other girls. Imagining angels delivering party invitations seemed to delight everyone.

"That's right, Tina. The shepherds were the first to hear the good news. God did not invite priests, or royalty, or nobility. Instead he reached down to simple men who would appreciate the honor they received.

"Somehow it seems appropriate that the shepherds received this privilege. Just imagine-Jesus who is often called the 'Good Shepherd' was first welcomed by them. He who was destined to be heaven's perfect sacrificial lamb was presented to the shepherds first."

"Wait a minute! You've missed the three kings! God invited them to his birthday party!" Mandy piped up.

"Actually that was another time and another place, Mandy."

June grinned at the flabbergasted reactions she received at her answer.

"The wise men have been added to the Christmas nativity scenes over the years just to condense the sequence of events, and to add the gift-giving aspect into the Christmas season."

Lauren whispered to Mandy, "That's my favorite aspect!"

"We'll get to the wise men soon enough. But first there were a few other events that unfolded in Mary's life."

* * * * *

I should be tired, Lord, but there's so much to think about, so much has happened.

After a long journey, a tiring labor and the final joy of your Son's birth I thought I would sleep for hours. I'd barely drifted into an exhausted slumber when I woke up.

I felt disoriented at first. There was a confusing onslaught to my senses. Unfamiliar smells, the poking of hay through the blanket I slept on, a rustling of animals stirring around us. Yet now a new sound crept into my mind, bringing me back from a restless sleep, fog-filled with the aftermath of pain and discomfort from childbirth. It was this new noise that roused me.

I felt Joseph rise from where he had been reclining next to me. He crept outside the cave, leaving his post of keeping watch over his new little family. I could hear his hushed voice replying to the sound of many excited whispers. I called out to him, wanting to know what the problem was. He came back to my side, a look of awe on his face as he quietly relayed the story brought by a group of shepherds who were outside.

They were asking to come in and see our Son. They said an angel had told them he was born and where to find him.

Joseph still seemed hesitant to let them in. He's already wearing the awesome responsibility of husband and new father perfectly. He was protective of my privacy, protective of your newborn baby, who lay so small and helpless.

"I'm fine, Joseph." I whispered to reassure him. Gazing at the sweet baby lying in the manger next to me, I smiled proudly back at Joseph. "If the angels told them to come, then they should come!"

Making sure I was comfortable and covered warmly with the blanket, Joseph went to invite the unexpected visitors into our humble surroundings.

Joseph returned, leading several men into the presence of your Son, Father. By their rough, unkempt appearance it was obvious they had been camping out on the hills with their flocks. But the look of awe and wonder in their eyes belied their outer appearance. They radiated an attitude of worship, glowing as though they had just returned from a sacred meeting with you, Father. These men, weathered by the elements, were at home amongst the animals, fitting more comfortably in our surroundings than many others could. They sank to their knees, encircling the manger where Jesus lay. A breathless silence held them in awe as they gazed at the precious form of your sleeping Son.

Their demeanor revealed an inner character of gentle tenderness. I watched amazed as tears formed and silently trailed down creased, toughened faces. The honor of receiving a heavenly invitation to this audience seemed to keep them immobile for an eternity. The moment was filled with a joy felt by each of us.

I overheard whispers shared between the shepherds kneeling in awe around the stone throne cradling your Son.

"It's just as the angel said. The baby's wrapped in swaddling cloths and lying in a manger!"

"What a perfect baby he is. Just like our own unblemished lambs!"

"It's an honor that we should see this child with our own eyes!"

They shared their excitement with us at the miraculous events they had witnessed that night. The words of the angels' song, 'Glory to God in the highest, and on earth peace to men on whom his favor rests!' were spoken over and over in hushed voices.

Father, it was a privilege to see their joy as they suddenly realized their worth in your eyes. Tonight these simple shepherds, often unable to worship in your synagogue because of being 'unclean,' felt that in your eyes they were clean enough to worship in the very presence of their newborn Messiah.

Joseph and I felt a different joy, knowing that the birth of your Son hadn't gone completely unnoticed. Indeed, from the shepherds' experience we learned there were angels singing and

I'm sure the great celebration of praise is still ringing throughout heaven.

Once again, Father, you've provided us the assurance that your hand is at work around us. We are living through something incredible. Lord, you are moving in mysterious ways to bring about the salvation of your people. It's wonderful to have a part in your plan.

Chapter Five – Simeon's Prophecy

"Do you see how God has been with Mary each step of this journey?" June paused in her narrative to summarize the events so far.

"God provided a place to stay with her cousin Elizabeth for three months while she waited to hear from Joseph. God provided the assurance Joseph needed to believe and take Mary as his wife. God used a political census to bring them to Bethlehem, the foretold birthplace of the Messiah. God provided a semi-private location for Jesus' birth. He provided a celebration and the assurance of his presence as the shepherds shared the angels' appearance with Mary and Joseph.

"There's a verse at this point that says, 'Mary treasured up all these things, pondering them in her heart.' Doesn't that make you wonder what kind of girl Mary was?"

"What does 'ponder' mean?" Tina queried.

"To think deeply, or to consider carefully. I suspect that when Mary was pondering, she was spending a lot of time talking things over with God. She must have wondered what it all meant, where God was leading them. I'm sure she had a walking prayer life."

"What do you mean, a 'walking prayer life'?"

"I simply mean that as you carry on throughout your day, God is included in your thoughts. You talk events over with Him. You're simply inviting God to be right there, walking beside you in your heart, soul and mind."

There was a quiet shuffling as the girls uncomfortable with these serious thoughts strove to ease the tension. Maria broke the silence, bringing everyone back to a more neutral ground.

"So what happens next? They can't leave Bethlehem, because the wise men haven't come yet. But they aren't going to stay in a barn!"

Heads nodded in agreement, as five pairs of enquiring eyes swiveled to June, awaiting her explanation.

"You're right, Maria, they didn't stay in the barn. It says that they were living in a house when the wise men did come. When the census was finished the flood of people returned to their hometowns. Joseph and Mary would've been able to find a nicer place to live.

"They didn't return to Nazareth right away because they had to travel the short distance to Jerusalem after the period of purification, which was to be made 40 days after a son was born. So the trip back to their hometown would have been put off until after that, or even longer, probably for a number of reasons.

"Nazareth was quite a distance from Bethlehem and wouldn't be an easy trip to make with a brand new baby. It was too soon and too dangerous to travel in small groups. Normally they would have traveled in a large group with all the others returning to their hometowns.

"For whatever reason, they decided to stay in Bethlehem. I'm sure Joseph was able to work as a carpenter while they remained there."

"Wait a minute." Rebecca held up a hand to halt Ms. June's narrative. "You said something about 'purification'. What's that all about?"

"I'm glad you brought that up, Rebecca. I almost missed an important event. Something amazing once again happened at that time. It was something which may have encouraged Mary, but also may have worried her."

"Worried her? What do you mean?" As usual Tina was first to pick up the emotional impact of events.

"First of all, the purification sacrifice is found in the Jewish law. It required a woman to present an offering at the temple 40 days after the birth of a son, or 60 days after the birth of a daughter, for her purification."

Tina's brow wrinkled in confusion as she asked, "So what's worrisome about that?"

"Nothing at all. This was a tradition they were used to and I'm sure everything went as expected. But while they were at the temple they had two encounters that may have left them questioning what God was going to do in their lives.

"The first encounter was with a man named Simeon. God had promised Simeon that he would not die until he had seen the Messiah. As soon as he saw Mary and Joseph with baby Jesus, he confronted them and took Jesus in his arms. He praised God, blessed the parents, but he also prophesied something that might have worried a new mother."

"Like what?" Mandy queried, leaning forward anxiously, for once forgetting to giggle.

"He told Mary that a sword would pierce her soul."

"That's a horrible thing to say!" Lauren gasped.

"He was simply proclaiming a prophecy from the Lord. I'm not sure I would've wanted to hear such a thing, but maybe it's better to be forewarned.

"They had barely stopped reeling from the impact of Simeon's words when another prophet, or in this case a prophetess, named Anna, also approached to see the baby. She too praised God for this child who would be God's redemption."

* * * * *

Father God, it has been a long, long day. I'm glad to be home! It's good that Joseph decided we should remain here in Bethlehem for a while. Today I truly appreciate the foresight he had in knowing how difficult it would be for me and baby Jesus to travel any distance right now.

The short trip to Jerusalem today has worn all of us out. Although some of the weariness I feel is from the dark cloud that seems to overshadow my mind right now.

Thank you, Lord, for the blessing of this tiny home we've been provided with. The innkeeper and his wife have been so welcoming. As soon as they heard that Joseph was a carpenter by trade, they jumped at the opportunity, asking him to work for them in return for us staying in the small house they own behind the inn. There appears to be no shortage of work for a carpenter right now. People have been happy to trade Joseph's skills at building and repair work for the provisions we need.

Father, I'm so tired right now. My emotions seem to be in a jumble of confusion all the time. Joy and excitement may reign, yet the tears are always there, like a water jar filled to the brim, ready to overflow at the slightest jostle. It's been an exhausting time these last few weeks since Jesus' birth. I was exhausted from childbirth, but I've healed and regained my strength. I was also exhausted from settling into our new home.

Yet none of those are the primary reason for my exhaustion.

Lord, have you noticed you have a very hungry Son? He seems to need nourishment and attention at all hours of the day! Truthfully, sleep is what I miss the most. But Father, what a joy and light he's brought into my life! The time I spend nursing, cleaning, talking and singing to Jesus is simply the most precious time I have experienced.

He is growing and filling out now. No longer the red wrinkled newborn, he's now a plump, soft baby, with fluffy dark curls that beg to be caressed and the most beautiful warm eyes that gaze up at me. I love your Son so much! More than I realized I would.

Lord, after today I'm confused and filled with dread. I love Jesus so much I can't bear to think that anything could harm him. What happened today at the temple in Jerusalem has me baffled.

Early this morning we started out, excited to be making the short trip to Jerusalem. Finally it was time for the purification sacrifice. I say 'short trip,' but with a baby not quite six weeks old, it seemed to take a great deal longer to do anything, including travel.

Upon reaching the temple, we purchased the doves for the sacrifice. Then it happened.

An old man made a sudden beeline across the temple courtyard, cutting across our path. When he reached out his arms to take Jesus from me, I was so startled I gripped him tighter to my chest. Poor Jesus woke up and gave a protesting squawk. My worries were laid to rest when Joseph reassured me, explaining that this was the holy man, Simeon. I relinquished my Son into his eager, outstretched arms.

Father, I was amazed at the joy that radiated from his face, sparkling in his aged eyes as they glistened with unshed tears of thanksgiving. He held our Son with reverent gentleness, truly knowing who it was he held in his arms.

Simeon raised his voice in praise. He said that finally your promise to him was fulfilled. Now he had seen your salvation, the salvation you prepared for all people through your Son. He blessed us. But I don't understand what he said next.

Father, he said Jesus was destined to cause the fall and rise of many, that he will be spoken against, and will reveal the thoughts and hearts of many. Finally Simeon turned to me and told me a sword would pierce my soul!

Tears sprang to my eyes at his words. I don't know what this means. I'm afraid to know what it may mean.

Before we could even respond or question Simeon further, a tiny old woman appeared at our side. She too began praising you, saying this was the child who would bring about redemption. We were told later that she is the prophetess Anna who has lived at the temple, worshipping, praying and fasting for years.

These two are your prophets, Father, and it was incredible to see you answer the prayers of these two faithful old servants of yours. I'm glad they've seen your Son and know who he is. But now my heart is heavy with a burden over what the future holds for this sweet innocent babe lying cradled, so trusting, in my arms.

Lord, if I could protect him from all harm, I would, but somehow I know you have a bigger plan and though I don't understand what that will mean, still I trust you. Father, please strengthen Jesus as he grows to complete your work.

And Father, I pray that you help me. I do not want to fail you or my Son. Give me strength through whatever may pierce my soul, as I see Jesus fulfill his destiny.

Chapter Six – First Steps

"Okay, we understand that Mary, Joseph and Jesus are still living in Bethlehem, in a house." Maria summarized, seeming anxious to move the story along. "So now do the wise men show up?"

"Well, yes they do, Maria." June replied.

As Maria sat back with a self-satisfied smirk, June couldn't resist teasing the girl by holding back a little longer.

With a twinkle in her eye, she added, "But…you should realize that Joseph, Mary and Jesus may have lived in Bethlehem for quite some time before the wise men arrived. In fact it could have been anywhere up to two years!"

"Two years!" Maria gasped.

"Yes, two years. Can you just imagine all that was happening while they lived in Bethlehem? Mary was probably a typical new mother. By that I mean, she must have felt a great deal of pride and excitement watching all the first experiences happening in Jesus' life. She was watching him grow from a newborn baby into a toddler. She was there as he learned to crawl, learned to feed himself, spoke his first word and took his first step."

* * * * *

Father, your Son is so beautiful!

I love kneeling here beside him as he sleeps in the afternoon. See his dark feathery eyelashes fluttering against plump cheeks, flushed and rosy in sleep. Do you know what he's dreaming? The excitement of this morning must be replaying in his mind.

Did you see him today, Lord? He walked! I laughed so hard at his waddling gait and clapped at his excitement. It was like watching an awkward bird try to take flight. Chortling with infectious laughter, he took his first steps. Chubby little legs were wobbling, arms out wide for balance, waving wildly, he looked ready to fly. Triumphant, he finally reached me and those tiny arms tightened, hugging my neck.

Swinging him up in my arms, we joyously danced, twirling round and round. Finally we tumbled to the ground, laughing so hard, unable to stand from dizziness and joy. Together we lay catching our breath, content to wait for the world to stop tilting crazily. His head tucked under my chin while soft ebony curls danced in the cooling breeze, tickling my cheek.

Burying my face in his silky curls I felt a wave of protectiveness wash over me at that sweet baby smell. Tightening my arms around his soft plump form, my spirit soared at the preciousness of this little boy I held. Father, so often I am overcome at the mystery of our Son and who he is. I still can't help but wonder who am I that you should choose me to be his mother, Lord. What an awesome privilege and awesome responsibility.

Lying there so content and joyous one minute, I suddenly found tears stinging my eyes as I continually ponder the future of this beloved Son. Through my worries I felt the warmth of his love flow over my spirit, comforting like soothing oil, pouring and wrapping around me like those little arms. What joy he has for life!

I can hardly wait till Joseph comes home. He'll be so proud. Now in a short matter of time, I know Jesus will want to follow him all over, toddling along, trying to be Daddy's big helper.

Our Son is growing up so quickly, Father. It seems like only yesterday he lay as a newborn babe, content in my arms, nursing at my breast. I remember vividly the velvet feel of his tiny hand against me. I would watch in wonder those perfect fingers curl, resting over my heart, as though taking comfort in its beating.

Each day I see the world you created through new eyes as I watch Jesus discover glorious wonders around him. Just yesterday he sat entranced, caressing the petal of a flower. His little fingers delicately explored the smooth textures, gently so as not to bruise its fragile form. He buried his nose in the bloom and sneezed as the pollen dusted his nose a bright yellow. I couldn't help but laugh at the comic look of surprise on his face followed by his sweet chuckle.

Is it my imagination, or is there recognition in his gaze as he sees each delight, as if he were reacquainting himself, rather than making a new discovery? Maybe I expect too much because I know how special he is. I know every mother I've met at the well will boast about her child, certain that theirs is the smartest, most special, wonderful child born. Yet in Jesus' case he is, for he is yours, Father.

Lord, how can I raise your Son when I'm so imperfect and sinful? I know you chose me, but I'm not sure I'm up to the task. If I could ask you for anything, Lord, I would ask for the gift of Solomon – wisdom. What can I teach the child who has come from the All-knowing One Himself? Do I dare discipline the Son of God? Or will he be perfect and not need my discipline? What a strange thought – a child who may need to discipline his parent.

Ah – he is stirring from his nap. Those little sighs he makes as he rouses from sleep always thrill me. I look forward to spending time together again, just him and me. Is it wrong to feel so jealous of our quiet times of communion together? Soon I know those beautiful eyes will open and look deep into mine. That look is like being absorbed into the deepest darkest pool of love. I'm sure he sees the farthest reaches of my soul and loves me completely.

Thank you, Lord. You chose me to be his mother, though I feel unworthy. Through our Son you've blessed me beyond description. Sweet little Jesus is my joy and I delight in everything about him. What a beautiful boy we have!

Chapter Seven – The Magi

"*D*on't worry, Maria, we've definitely come to the wise men."

June smiled as Rebecca and Maria muttered, "Finally!" in unison.

"First, why don't you girls tell me what you know about the wise men?"

June held her breath in anticipation. She watched Mandy and Lauren sit up, suddenly alert, winding up for their usual ping pong match of answers.

"There were three."

"They were kings."

"They came from the east…"

"…following a star…"

"…and brought gifts of gold…"

"…frankincense and myrrh…"

"…and they traveled on camels…"

"…camels, that probably stank!" Lauren added triumphantly, getting in the final word.

June finally released her breath in a sigh and smiled as she tried to replay the list of answers at normal instead of hyper speed for everyone.

"Well, the Bible doesn't tell us how many wise men there were.

People take it for granted that because there were three gifts then there must have been three wise men. There was more than one, but otherwise we don't know how many. They were coming from the east, but the Bible seems to call them Magi, or traditionally Wise Men, not necessarily kings, no matter what the Christmas carol calls them. The three gifts you mentioned, gold, frankincense and myrrh would have been valuable, deserving of a king. These men were obviously men of great wealth and probably revered in their own country. It's likely they traveled by caravan on camels, and with an entourage of servants for this long a trip."

"What about the star, Ms. June?" Tina spoke up.

"Yes, Tina, we can't forget the star. These wise men were astrologers who studied the heavens. The appearance of this bright star in the night sky was significant to them. They read it as a sign that a king had been born in Israel. So they packed up their caravan, put together gifts worthy to present to royalty and made the long journey to honor the newborn king."

"They followed it to Bethlehem, right?" Tina interjected.

"First they followed it to Jerusalem, because that's where they naturally expected the king to be born. The priests in Jerusalem told them about the prophecy that foretold the Messiah would be born in Bethlehem. So they carried on with their journey to Bethlehem and the star led them to the house where Mary and Jesus were."

* * * * *

Father, I don't know what to think about the events of last evening and today. What amazing visitors you brought to our humble home!

Yesterday, the early evening was promising a beautiful clear night sky. After supper little Jesus was anxious to get outside the stuffy confines of our small home. He wanted to enjoy the refreshing breeze while gazing in wonder as evening stars blinked on while dusk settled in.

Outside, he sat contentedly on my lap, giggling as I bounced him and quoted our favorite praise verses to the lilting rhythm of each bounce.

Then there it was again! The most incredible star lit up the heavens. We had admired its beauty every night for months. Once again it was the first to point down at us.

"Ooo! Mine! My 'tar."

Jesus' chubby little arms lifted, reaching up to touch the starlight beaming down upon us.

"Yes, little one," I smiled at our game. "That's your pretty star."

We had played out this little scenario many times over the months while living here in Bethlehem. Even when a few months old, before he could babble any words that made sense, Jesus would reach up, waving wildly with delight at the appearance of the bright heavenly beacon.

I would tell him, "Star, that's a star!"

He would turn his beautiful eyes towards me and I could see the star's reflection sparkle in them.

Next I would ask, "Who made the star?"

He'd wave wildly at the heavens, giggling, and cooing.

Nodding my head, as though understanding those baby noises, I would reply, "That's right – your Father God made the star!"

I remember clearly one special evening when Jesus was several months old. We were repeating our performance, pointing out the sparkling star, when suddenly he exclaimed, "'tar, mine!"

The words were so clear! It was precious to hear him claim ownership of one of your heavenly creations, Lord. As heir of our Creator, I allowed him to claim the beautiful diamond resting above us.

From that day on, we looked for the star each evening, many times with Joseph at our side if he was home from his carpentry work. It was a joy to hear the childish voice starting to learn language. We marveled that a young child, barely able to walk, could communicate so well, with actions, and a few garbled sounds that were becoming words we could understand.

But once again everything has changed. It's hard to believe it happened only last night. I remember sitting in this very spot, little realizing the surprise you were bringing to us, Lord. Our nightly star game played out so differently and now my view and understanding of that star has completely changed.

As usual, last night, Jesus' little arms had lifted, reaching up to touch the starlight. He once again claimed ownership.

"Oh! Mine! My 'tar!'"

We'd barely finished this little ritual when I heard the unmistakable clopping of several pack animals, the jingling and creaking of harnesses and leather straps stretching as packs swayed with the motion of their animal carriers. A caravan at this time of the evening was unusual enough, but, Lord, when they stopped in front of our house I was shocked and frightened.

I grasped Jesus in my arms protectively and looked up at these strangers, dressed in such odd fashion. Even the darkening night sky could not hide that these were men of wealth, accompanied by many servants. It was obvious the travelers were from a country far away. Atop the perch of their saddles, they sat momentarily silent, staring down at Jesus.

As I arose, ready to flee to a neighbor's house, or call out for help, they dismounted and knelt down in front of us. I almost *dropped Jesus, as he struggled, desperately trying to get down. I can't explain why, but as I gazed at these strangers bowing in reverence, a sudden peace descended upon me. Somehow I knew you were there, Lord, and there was nothing to fear from these men.*

I set Jesus down to stand on his own and he toddled over to explore those who knelt before him. They heard his chatter and giggles, and at the touch of his little hands, exploring the rich textures of their robes, they lifted their heads and looked over at me with awe and wonder written in their expressions.

"We have followed his star," they explained.

At the word 'star,' Jesus looked up into the night sky, waving his hands excitedly at the sparkling gem shining down and exclaimed, "Mine!"

Though I no longer felt threatened at the strangers' appearance, I was relieved as I saw Joseph hurrying up the road, to my side. He placed an arm around me in a protective stance but was too surprised to speak. Together we gazed at the unusual guests who knelt before Jesus in such reverence. The explanation for their sudden appearance on our doorstep seemed almost odder than anything else that had happened to us since Jesus' coming had been announced by angelic visitors.

"It was foretold that a star in the east would lead us to the one who would be born as King of the Jews. We have come to worship him and honor him with our gifts."

Dear God, we didn't know what to say. Wordlessly we stood, overwhelmed by their presence and what they were saying. With humble ceremony they placed three gifts before Jesus. They were gifts befitting a king - gold, frankincense and myrrh.

Finally, I was able to offer them a drink of water after their long dusty journey. I could hardly believe we were entertaining such no-

bility. Joseph sat with our honored guests who seemed unable to keep their eyes from little Jesus. Here he was at last, their goal, the prize finally reached. Their search for the foretold king was over.

Their story was of a long journey, leading first to Jerusalem, where they were sure the king would be born. While searching there they were informed by priests of the prophecy which foretold that the king would be born in Bethlehem. At the mention of the prophecy, Lord, I marveled at how you brought it to pass. I find it amazing that it was fulfilled. You brought unexpected circumstances about so that Jesus would be born here instead of where we had expected, at our home in Nazareth.

As the visitors' story continued, my heart dropped when they told of their audience with King Herod. They seemed joyful that Herod had said his desire was to worship this king as well. At this claim my eyes met Joseph's and I could see from his expression that he was worried also. This was not like the King Herod we had heard about. Herod had had his own sons killed because he thought they would take his throne from him!

That night the regal travelers set up their tents and camped in the fields behind the homes of Bethlehem. Their plan was to return through Jerusalem in order to report back to Herod.

Joseph and I barely slept. Our minds were occupied with both the evening's excitement and a dark cloud of worry that weighed on our hearts. It was a long night spent talking over the events that had occurred and praying for your guidance and protection, Father.

This morning the caravan once more stopped on their way out of town and they told us that a heavenly visitor had warned them not to return to Jerusalem. They were on their way home by another route.

Thank you, Lord, for you answered the concerns Joseph and I

had about King Herod. O Lord, what a relief to know that you are still protecting us. We waved farewell as we watched the unusual procession wind its way down the road.

Now it's evening once again as Jesus and I sit here admiring your heavens. Yet this time I wonder at the mystery of Jesus' star and the way even your heavens announced the birth of your Son. I'm amazed, Lord, as I realize how close to the truth our evening star game had come. As Jesus had claimed so many times, that star truly was 'My 'tar!'."

Chapter Eight – Fleeing to Egypt

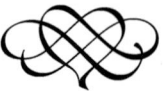

"Wait a minute! You forgot the part about King Herod." Maria straightened up, seeming pleased to catch an omission.

"King Herod," June shook her head sadly, "He must have been completely mad. He caused a great deal of grief."

"When King Herod heard the wise men were asking around for the whereabouts of the new king, he tried to trick them into returning to him once this new king was located. He said he wanted to worship the new king, but we know he planned to have him killed. History tells us that Herod was so jealous of his throne he even had some of his own sons murdered because he thought they were out to steal it from him. Fortunately, God proved once again that he is the great Provider and Protector."

"How'd he do that?" Tina asked anxiously.

"God sent his angel to warn the Magi not to return to Jerusalem. Instead they returned to their homeland by another route."

"I bet that made Herod mad!" Lauren piped up.

"Madder than he already was, that is." Mandy added.

"Indeed, it angered Herod so much when he realized he had been tricked that he decided he would get rid of that king, no matter what the cost. Fortunately the Lord sent an angel in a dream to warn Joseph that he should wake his family and immediately escape to Egypt, out of reach of the vengeful king. I like to think the gifts from the wise men were God's way of providing for their needs as they quickly left everything and settled in another country for a year or so."

*   *   *   *   *

Father, it's still hours before dawn. I'm so tired, but I thank you that little Jesus has slept so well during this tumultuous night.

Joseph seems energized with urgency, trying to put as much distance between ourselves and Bethlehem. Could it be only a few short hours have passed since he awoke from the dream? He said it was a warning brought by your angelic messenger. He shot upright so quickly from his sleep that he startled me awake.

"Mary, we must hurry and leave this place. At once. Tonight. Immediately! I've been warned by God's angel. Jesus is in danger from Herod. We're leaving now! Start packing. I'll fetch our donkey from the stable."

Without question, I arose quietly, so as not to wake our sleeping Son. My hands trembled at this new threat. I rolled our sleeping pallets, and gathered what food items I could bag up to carry for our trip.

Where are we to go, Lord? That question kept repeating in my mind as I hurried with the packing. How far away can we travel to be outside the reach of Herod and his soldiers?

Silently, Joseph and I worked together, packing the donkey with only the bare essentials that we could take with us.

As I mounted, shifting a sleeping Jesus securely in my arms, I looked back with sorrow. I knew we were saying goodbye to the tiny home we'd been happy in. Though a simple dwelling, it had become a cozy retreat, filled with the love and joy of our little family. Many of the homey touches were being left behind as nonessentials. So many memories of our lives spent in the town of Jesus' birth.

Bethlehem had been a small haven for us to begin anew. We had been welcomed and Joseph was given the chance to ply his carpentry skills for many who lived there. He hadn't earned a lot, but enough work was available to provide us with a home and basic necessities. The friendship and acceptance offered from those we lived amongst is what I'll miss the most.

Leaving without saying goodbye to our friends and neighbors seems wrong. It felt as though we were stealing away, like thieves taking a precious treasure with us. That treasure is our Son. I know we're not leaving as thieves, but as protectors, keeping him from those who would rob us of his sacred life. Lord, why must this happen? How can men of this world be so cruel and evil?

Walking through the sleeping streets of Bethlehem, we tried to keep our passage quiet. As we passed each home I remember thinking of those sleeping inside, resting peacefully, unaware of the storm brewing around them. These people had welcomed and befriended us over the last year. Many we had grown to love.

As we left the town behind my mind was occupied with memories, the one luxury I could pack along.

Each morning, I loved meeting with the women as we gathered together at the well. The morning ritual of filling water jars at the town's well, was our opportunity to visit. I know it's a pleasure I won't experience here again. Amongst our small community of women, we shared our pride in our children. We'd watch and marvel as our babies and children grew, boasting of their achievements. Having no mother I could turn to here, I cherished the willingness of others who would pass on their wisdom and knowledge. As a new mother, I valued their advice about the many worries and questions of child-rearing. I still smile at the memory of friendly arguments that would inevitably arise over which plants were best to treat rashes and various ailments.

The children would play, running or crawling around their mother's feet. I can see clearly all the faces of those little ones Jesus learned to walk with and played with. Now they're left behind. I'm sure he'll miss their presence as much as I will their mothers.

While thinking of our friends I'm hit with a new worry. What'll happen when Herod's soldiers arrive in Bethlehem? Do they know who it is they are seeking? Will his anger lash out on our innocent friends and neighbors?

"I fear for the families we're leaving behind," I whisper to Joseph, breaking the silence we've held since our journey began, even though the homes disappeared many miles behind. Joseph tries to comfort and reassure my whispered concern.

"It'll be better for the others if they don't know where we've gone."

Joseph says he believes it's best this way. The soldiers won't be able to follow our trail, for no one knows where we've disappeared to. At least that's what he's saying to reassure me, but, Lord, I can tell that he's also concerned for their safety. Watch over Bethlehem and all who live there, Father.

The jolting gait of our donkey awakens memories of another trip made many months before. I find myself once again traveling on the donkey, but this time I am carrying my sleeping child in my *arms. Rather than birthing pains, I experience only the awkward gait of the donkey causing bruises from the jolting and the numbness in my arms and shoulders from the weight of cradling my beloved Son.*

Gazing down at his precious face, so beautiful and innocent in sleep, I can't help but wonder. How could anyone want to hurt him? My grip tightens around him protectively. He's getting heavy in my arms but I'm trying not to shift him too much for fear it might wake him. Though we appear to be alone out here on the trail, I don't want his crying to alert any creatures, animal or human, to our presence as we pass through the night.

Father, guide us safely on this journey. Joseph says we dare not head north back to Nazareth. He feels it's wiser to head for Egypt, outside Herod's reach. We can stay in the Jewish community near the border of Judea, just inside the land of Egypt. We should be able to live there until Herod is no longer a threat to Jesus.

Once again we face another journey, a new direction in our lives. I pray, Lord, that you continue to be our Guide along this new branch we are taking.

Though the sky is starlit, the night feels unfriendly. Shadows seem to be lurking, moving and shifting as we pass rocky outcrops. Sounds of night creatures hunting, strange whispers of the wind whipping through rocks and trees, keep us alert to possible dangers on the road.

Lord, it's only because of your warning that we'd even consider traveling in the dark. On any other night this would be a foolish trek to make. All the stories heard about highway robbers flood my mind. Many dangers lurk to catch the unsuspecting traveler. Danger can spring from thieves, from wild animals, or even something as simple as a misplaced footstep along the narrow rocky trail. A fall in the dark could lead to a crippling or fatal end to this trip.

Father, I rely on your guidance and protection right now. It makes me nervous knowing how vulnerable we are. Except I know you're with us. I know we're accompanied by the strongest ally of all.

You've reminded me of the beautiful shepherd song written by our beloved King David. Father, somehow I feel reassured and at peace as I rework this song into our circumstances.

> Lord, You are our shepherd. You have called us to follow you.
> You provide for our needs and help us find peace in green pastures.
> You will restore us again.
> Though we walk through the darkness, surrounded by threats of death,
> We fear no evil, for You are with us.
> Your strength protects us and we are comforted.
> You have prepared a place for us and will guide us there safely.
> Surely Your goodness and love will remain with us all the days of our lives
> As we dwell in Your presence forever, Lord.

Thank you, my heavenly Shepherd.

Chapter Nine – Weeping for the Babies

"So after they fled to Egypt, everything was all right?" Tina's voice held a hopeful note.

She knows the answer, June realized. It's as if she's hoping that by some miracle this time around the story might change. Sighing, June looked into those innocent eyes that pled for her to make it all right. Shaking her head sadly, she continued the lesson.

"For Mary, Joseph and Jesus, it was a miraculous rescue. They escaped and were safe in Egypt where they lived in a Jewish settlement that was there at the time.

"Unfortunately, there was no miracle for the town of Bethlehem and its surrounding area. Herod was furious when he realized the wise men had tricked him. He calculated from the time the Magi said the star had appeared in the sky and he commanded that every male child, two years of age and under, be killed.

"All of the baby boys and young toddlers were slaughtered. Even in those violent days, his edict must have been considered monstrous. I'm sure shock was felt throughout the whole nation as ripples of suffering and grief rocked the area.

"The news probably traveled all the way to Egypt where Mary and Joseph were bound to hear about it."

In the hushed silence, a tear openly trailed down Tina's cheek. The other girls lowered their heads, hiding their own glistening eyes. The only movement for the moment was a furtive hand or two wiping at the excess wetness. The class remained quiet as young minds tried to grasp the enormity of the act.

* * * * *

Dear Father, I feel sick. I'm sick in body, soul and spirit.

Once again I lie here, wakened and shivering from the nightmare that keeps coming back. Even while awake, just closing my eyes brings images and heartrending cries ringing in my ears.

'Dear God, help!'

'No, don't hurt my baby!'

Those words keep repeating over and over. Nausea washes over me each time my mind pictures Herod's soldiers grabbing the babies, snatching them from their mother's arms-all those sweet little boys we watched growing up in Bethlehem.

It's the middle of the night, but I've got to creep over to check on Jesus, just to reassure myself that he is safe. I want to pick him up and hug him tightly, but I know I shouldn't wake him. Still, just to watch him sleeping helps calm my soul.

A caravan of travelers brought the news from Bethlehem. It's hard to believe the horror and tragedy we left behind. Father, I can't stop crying for the loss of those little ones. I feel the weight of sorrow of mothers and fathers, empty arms reaching for sons who are no longer there to hold.

Do they hate us? Do they realize it was Jesus that Herod was seeking to kill? It's difficult to realize they're suffering from a tragedy we barely escaped. Your warning came soon enough for us to flee to safety, Lord, and for that I'm grateful. But Father, how could this happen? Why did all those innocent lives have to be taken, all that innocent blood spilt? It seems senseless, such a waste of life and purity.

When I first heard the news, many familiar faces paraded through my mind. Those of women friends gathering around the well, their children running, babies crawling, pulling up on a mother's skirt to stand, proud of their achievement. There are many faces and all of them were special to us. I can't believe how many of Jesus' playmates are gone.

I feel a burden of guilt. It weighs on my mind, that we might have been partly responsible. But I'm also overwhelmed by the realization that if we had stayed, Jesus would have been just one more victim of Herod's madness. I am so torn. I feel relieved that we weren't there, and yet sad that we can't be there to comfort our friends in their grief. Yet what comfort could we offer them now? They may despise us, for our Son is safe and alive.

Jesus is sleeping so peacefully. He's enjoying the rest of an innocent child, completely unaware of how close evil came to taking his life. How easily he could've been snatched from us! Will it always be this way? Will we always have to guard and protect him from this violent world we live in?

How soft Jesus' hair is. Caressing his sleeping head, I smile as a fleecy curl gently encircles my finger, clinging like one of the hugs he loves to give. I can't take my eyes off his sleeping form. These past few days I haven't wanted him out of my sight. My hand still shakes as I reach down to touch his precious little fingers.

Once again I close my tired eyes. Flashbacks from the nightmare appear burned behind my eyelids. I shiver with cold as images replay. The recurring dream is too vivid, the feeling of horror too real. It keeps repeating over and over. Everything is red, everywhere I look is splattered chaos, choking dust, terrified screams! Heartrending cries continue to echo in my mind. Not only my dreams but even my waking thoughts are haunted.

Opening my eyes, I gasp aloud, trying to shake off the chilling horror. Trying to dry my eyes, I watch a single tear escape to splash on the rosy cheek of our beloved Son. It almost looks like he's crying. Father, you're crying for those innocent ones, aren't you?

I've heard that Herod hasn't continued to search for the 'baby king'. He must feel he has wiped out another possible threat to that blood-soaked throne he fiercely protects. Thank you for your protection from such a monster.

Jesus' perfect little fingers wrap around mine with such trust, even in his sleep. I dare not let him see me cry for he wouldn't understand why and he'd be upset to see my anguish. Lord, I'm comforted, knowing you are guiding and protecting us. In the face of such dangers, thank you for your presence.

Help me turn these nightmares over to you, Lord. I pray that you would comfort those who are hurting. Heal their broken hearts. Hold those little boys in your arms, Lord, and give them the pure love that can only come from you. Their sacrifice helped protect your Son.

The bloodshed of the innocent is always the hardest to bear or understand. Even the temple sacrifice of unblemished lambs, the spilling of innocent blood, as called for in Your law, to bring us back into right relationship with you, Lord, is hard to bear. Somehow I never get used to the evil in this world, our sins, being paid for by the sacrifice of innocence!

Father, forgive us.

Chapter Ten-Nazareth

"How long did they live in Egypt?" Rebecca asked, being first to compose herself.

From the shifting and straightening in their seats, the others appeared grateful to be leaving the images from Bethlehem behind. Understanding their feelings, June willingly continued with the story.

"We're not exactly sure how long they lived there. It could have been a year, or possibly a couple of years. But they remained there in safety until God sent an angel to Joseph. He was told in a dream that Herod was dead and no further danger to Jesus. It was time for them to return to Israel."

"So now they go back to Nazareth, right?" Maria asked.

"Yes, that's right," June responded. "They entered Israel through the Judean countryside. When they heard that one of Herod's remaining sons had taken the throne, they realized he was as evil as his father. It was then they decided to head north to Galilee, making their way back to their hometown of Nazareth. After an absence of three or four years, they were finally coming home to settle down, to live and work and raise a family."

*　　*　　*　　*　　*

Nazareth! Finally, after so many years and so many miles, we're home at last. O Father, I'm happy to be with our families once more! The acceptance from our friends and family was overwhelming.

It seems unreal. Your angel told us King Herod was dead and it was safe to return to Israel. We were filled with relief and joy! Yet, I couldn't help but feel nervous as well.

Nevertheless I was happy to be packing our belongings for the journey. I'd never felt completely at home in Egypt, even living in a community of our own people. It was exciting to be returning to our own homeland, but it was an excitement filled with misgivings.

As we entered Judea the people we questioned told us Herod's son, Archelaus, was now reigning there. It is rumored that he is no different than his father. To be on the safe side, we decided to make the longer journey back to Galilee, returning to our hometown of Nazareth. That led to new misgivings. What would our reception there be like? Would people accept us? Would there still be whispers about Jesus' conception?

Now I laugh, Father, as I think of what truly happened. The joyful reception from those we've missed, and who've missed us, was greater than I could have hoped for. Jesus has been embraced with open arms. But how could they not love your Son? He is such a sweet child. He wins the hearts of everyone he meets. I've seen the hardest character melt under the clear purity of his gaze. Locking eyes with Jesus is to see his face light up with joy. It's as though he's looking deep into your soul and loving you intensely.

Father, it's also been good for Joseph to get back to his workshop. The people in town are clamoring for his carpentry skills. Thank you, Lord, for he is encouraged by all the business overflowing from his shop. He had been worried, but I told him he'd be busy. After all he is the best carpenter to be found anywhere. He has an artist's gift for working the wood, creating some of the strongest and most beautiful pieces. Even the simplest stool or table he creates has a symmetrical beauty about them.

I'm so proud of Joseph, Lord. You truly blessed me with a husband whom I can respect for many reasons-his talents, his integrity, his leadership in our family, his love and devotion to you. Truly he has been a wonderful father to your Son. Thank you for this husband who loves and cherishes me. I feel unworthy of such devotion sometimes, but I am grateful for him.

Lord, you have proven yourself over and over. I know that you've been with us each step of the journey. You are my Guide, my Protector and, as always, my Father God.

Chapter Eleven – A Special Friend

"*M*s. June, do you suppose…" Tina's voice faded, a blush stained her cheeks as she realized how her question might sound.

Trying to catch her downcast eyes, June smiled encouragingly.

"What is it, Tina? What do you want to suppose?"

"Well, it seems silly, but I was just wondering if you thought Jesus would have met other kids who were, well, you know…?"

"No, I don't know. What do you mean?" June prodded gently, wanting to understand what was causing such an agony of embarrassment to Tina.

Shifting uncomfortably in her beanbag chair, Tina glanced quickly to the side at Maria and Rebecca before proceeding.

"Like…well, I guess you could say…like me. Kind of, you know, different, or slow?" Tina's voice ended in a whisper, a flood of red seemed to infuse her face as she bowed her head in shame at her own shortcomings.

June ached to give the shrinking girl a huge hug, when to her surprise both Rebecca and Maria reached out to pat the shoulder and caress the curls of her bowed head.

"Don't say that, Tina!" Rebecca looked shocked at Tina's admission.

June watched the little drama unfold as Rebecca suddenly turned toward Maria. Both pairs of eyes widened in shock. Their shared look seemed to open a door of understanding. As realization brought a blush to their cheeks, they saw clearly how their actions had reinforced the shame Tina was feeling.

"I'm sorry if we made you feel that way, Tina." Maria whispered her apology and got up from her beanbag chair to kneel beside Tina. "You're the sweetest person we know and you don't deserve to feel that way."

"Yeah, next time we do or say something that makes you feel that way, well, you just whack us across the head. It might knock some sense into us!" Rebecca's outburst and accompanying smack to her own forehead brought chuckles from the girls.

Tina raised her head and shyly smiled at Rebecca's antics.

"I couldn't do that!" She exclaimed, although a twinkle in her eyes made June wonder if she wouldn't like to try.

"You've brought up an interesting supposition, Tina." June brought the class back to attention. "It could be possible that Jesus, as a child, met other children with various handicaps or disabilities, both physical and mental."

"What would he have been like to them, do you suppose?" Tina's eyes became wistful as she tried to imagine such a meeting.

"Well, I think Jesus would have been their best friend!" Lauren burst out staunchly.

"You're probably right, Lauren." June nodded at her idea. "Jesus loved everyone. He was full of compassion and spent much of his time reaching out to the unloved, the unaccepted, helping the sick and downtrodden. I'm sure he was just as loving and compassionate as a child too."

* * * * *

Father God, I'm amazed at the new lessons I keep learning from our young Son.

This morning, as usual, I gathered with the other mothers, collecting water from the well. We were idly visiting, not in a rush to return to our homes and unending chores. We enjoy the chance to laugh and share stories of our little ones. It's so cool in the morning and the children always have such fun running, chasing each other around the grassy area.

As I watched Jesus speak with his special friend Matthew, I was reminded of an incident that happened on a similar morning several days back. None of the mothers speak of it, but I know most of us were affected, almost as much as the children themselves.

On that morning Miriam was there as usual, with her son Matthew. I'd always felt sorry for her, having a child who seems like he'll never be more than a child. He's older than the other children who gather to play by the well. He's beyond the age where the boys begin their schooling at the synagogue. Yet everyone knows school will never be an option for him. He is farther behind most of the young children in his speech and even his movements are those of an awkward child having just learned to walk. Matthew's name, which means "Gift of God," always seemed to be a sad joke to many people, maybe even to Miriam and her husband.

The usual games of chase were happening that day, when a commotion broke out amongst the children. All us mothers were distracted from our visiting and turned to see what the ruckus was about.

There Matthew stood, large and lanky, surrounded by a circle of small tormentors. They marched around him, laughing and pointing, mocking his ungainly walk, imitating his slurred speech. Matthew's head was bowed, his eyes squeezed tight, trying to stop the tears from falling. His hands covered ears that burned at the shouts and laughter. Stooped shoulders shook silently in sorrow, hunched against the taunts.

Aghast, I turned towards Miriam. Embarrassed, she had turned her back on the scene. Tears of humiliation and a rush of red flooding her cheeks told of the conflict she felt. She knew everyone, even the children, judged her son as worthless. The weight of their judgment seemed to rest on her and her husband also, for many believed only terrible sinners would have given birth to such a child.

Suddenly, in the background, I saw Jesus approach the group of children. Dark eyes flashed a molten look of stony determination that I'd never seen on his young face before. Though smaller than many in the group, the circle broke open for him, dividing like the Red Sea did for our people. He proudly stood next to Matthew, his head barely reaching the older boy's shoulder. Reaching up, he placed a comforting hand on Matthew's shaking shoulder.

A sudden silence fell amongst the children. Jesus' direct look touched each child in turn. Like a candle sputtering out, the gleeful teasing left their eyes and each child looked away. A wave of shame washed over them, dissolving the circle of mockers until only the two of them stood there.

Jesus turned to Matthew, who stood there, shoulders hunched, head bowed, hiding his tear-stained face. Raising his hands, Jesus cupped Matthew's cheeks, forcing the bowed head to meet his eyes.

"God made you, Matthew, and God doesn't make mistakes. You're special to Him and you're special to me. Never forget you're loved!"

O Father, the older boy's head came down on Jesus' shoulder and his loud sobs could be heard everywhere. Those two remained locked together in an awkward hug of friendship that seemed to heal the spirit of a young lad who had suffered his whole life.

It may have been that he was sobbing out emotions that had weighed on him since birth. Maybe he shed tears for feeling unloved. Maybe he sobbed at being an embarrassment to his parents. Maybe he simply cried at the confusion of being mocked. But, Lord, I feel his was a healing cry of relief and joy. Finally he was feeling love and acceptance in the hug of our little Son's arms. No longer was he a person with no value. In one morning, that changed forever.

The power in Jesus' simple words, spoken in his sweet childlike voice, will stay with me always. I know it has with Matthew and Miriam.

Today I watched Matthew running, still awkwardly, but with such freedom. Now joy shines in his eyes because he knows he is loved. Many times Matthew follows Jesus around, not wanting to talk, for that's still difficult for him, but simply to see the miracle of love in Jesus' eyes. In that gaze he sees himself reflected as someone special. From Jesus he always receives the gift he craves from a friend, a smile and a hug.

Miriam also seems more at ease and filled with joy. Her eyes now watch Matthew with such love and there's peace in her face. Finally she has realized that she can be proud of her son. He truly is her Matthew, her 'gift from God'.

Once again our little boy has given me much to think about. Like Jesus said, "God doesn't make mistakes."

Chapter Twelve – A Sunset

"Hey, Ms. June, I have another 'do you suppose' question!" Mandy sat up loosening the pillows of her couch nest.

"What would you like to suppose, Mandy?" June asked, smiling at the excitement that glowed from the young faces around her.

The idea of Jesus experiencing everyday life and problems as he grew up seemed to suddenly have their imaginations working overtime.

"Do you suppose Jesus had problems with his parents? Did Mary or Joseph ever get mad at him?"

"That's an interesting thought, Mandy," June mused. "We know that Jesus was without sin, but that didn't mean that his parents were. I'm sure there were days when Mary might have been overtired and overworked as any mother can become, and she may have become impatient with her children, including Jesus."

"I wonder what Jesus would have done?" Mandy mused. "I mean if my mom gets mad at me and I'm not doing anything wrong, I get really upset and we usually end up yelling or arguing over something stupid!"

Maria shook her head knowingly. "Well, I don't think Jesus would have yelled at his mother. I mean I just can't see that happening! One of the Ten Commandments says to honor your father and mother. So yelling at her, even if he hadn't done anything wrong, wouldn't be very honoring, would it?"

"No...I don't suppose so." Mandy's mouth pursed as she recalled her own reactions to her mother.

"Maria, you have a good point." June jumped into the thoughtful pause. "I'm sure Jesus showed honor to his parents, even if they became impatient or upset. Maybe he looked past their outward behavior and realized their outburst was caused by something other than him."

"So what you're saying is I shouldn't jump to defend myself by yelling and arguing?" Mandy looked at June, searching for some practical answers.

"I guess not. Has anything been accomplished from that response so far?" At the vehement shaking of Mandy's head, June continued. "Then I suppose if we can halt our first reaction, pause and think, 'What would Jesus have done?' maybe we can cool down the situation before it escalates and feelings get hurt. It's not an easy thing to do when we feel unjustly accused, but I believe if we ask for God's strength and wisdom, we can learn to honor our parents even at times like that."

* * * * *

Father God, forgive my impatience. I told you I was weak and unworthy. How forgiving and loving is this young man of ours.

As I watch Jesus, I realize that soon he'll be considered a man. He's nearly twelve, but I can close my eyes and still see my baby, my little boy growing up, dancing and playing, enjoying life's simple pleasures. Yet what wisdom and maturity he's always surprising me with! I've learned so much from him, so much in fact that many times I feel he's the parent and I'm the child. Today was one of those learning days.

As happens too often, I let the busy-ness of life overwhelm me. When evening approached, I felt I had too much to do and not enough help. I was wearing a path in the floor, pacing from table to window to door, waiting for sight of Jesus returning home from some errands I had asked him to take care of.

I was muttering under my breath, grumbling that, as usual, he was being too slow. I could see in the expressions of my other children that they thought I was being unreasonable. Still it didn't stop me. Somehow my impatience needed a scapegoat and it was Jesus. Though his younger sisters and brothers were making an effort to help, it didn't seem to be quite good enough. It was Jesus' help I thought I needed. So reasonable or not, he had become my target.

"That boy, he'll stop to admire every blade of grass, or flowering weed, or pay heed to every neighbor's woes if I don't prod him along! When will he learn to just do what has to be done and come home immediately?" I snapped aloud, as I finally stomped out of the house to look for him.

I continued my mental grumbling, 'I can't believe that I have to take the time to hurry him home.'

I followed the well-worn pathway that I knew he would take. On the way I practiced a few choice words that would bring just the right amount of guilt, as only a mother can do. Anyone watching would have surely thought a mad woman was stomping past them, muttering aloud to herself and gesturing wildly.

At last I saw him through the trees, and even before coming completely in sight, I started my routine.

"Jesus! Why do you have to dawdle, when I need your help? Don't you think I have better things to do than wait for you?" The

sharp edge in my voice dripped with sarcasm. Lord, I blush even now as I think about it.

There he stood, on the little rise, still and silent overlooking the view, watching the sky set into its evening glory. As my harsh cry destroyed the reverent silence, he turned and looked at me. That look humbled me; it crushed my angry spirit.

His look was filled with awe and wonder. It spoke of the joy and communion he found with you, Lord, through your creative masterpiece. He was worshipping you, Father, and I felt so ashamed at my anger and impatience.

I felt like a nagging mother who had just stormed into the synagogue, screaming out during a Sabbath service. I started to cry in remorse and embarrassment. I wanted to turn and hide my shame. Words couldn't get past the lump in my throat. Through the tears, my eyes pled for Jesus to forgive me.

He just smiled that smile I love so much. All his love for me was held in that smile and poured over into his dark eyes, so full of warmth and forgiveness. Holding out a hand to me, he whispered with quiet reverence.

"Take just a minute and stay with me, Mother. Let's watch the glorious picture Father is painting for us."

It felt like we stood on holy ground. Slowly we knelt side by side. I don't know how long we remained there, hand in hand, transfixed as you mixed and stroked the heavens with color. We watched them meld from gold, to all the colors of fire, darkening to deepest garnet and finally the royal blue of a night sky.

In silence we walked back toward the house, his hand on my shoulder in sweet companionship. Finally, while peering from the corner of his eyes, he answered the question I had snapped earlier about having better things to do than wait for him.

"You know, Mom," his eyes twinkled, easing the reproof and turning it into a gentle reminder, "if you learn to 'wait upon the Lord,' He will renew your strength."

I was once again amazed at his wisdom. He always seems to know just what I need to hear. With a simple quote from your prophet Isaiah, Jesus had reminded me of what is important, Father. I knew it was truth he spoke, for I felt energized and rejuvenated after our quiet worship time on the hillside. My soul surely had soared like an eagle in worship of You, O Lord.

Once again I'm ending this day humbled as I see our Son's maturity. I am challenged to be more like Jesus, learning to rest in you each moment, just as he does.

Chapter Thirteen – A Lost Son

"You know," June paused thoughtfully, "there was one time mentioned in the Bible where it appears Mary was frustrated and got upset with Jesus when he was a young man."

"Really?! When?" Mandy sat up, dislodging the pillows once again from her nesting corner.

"It happened after Jesus had turned twelve years old. He would now be considered a man in Jewish society. This was the first time he was finally able to travel to Jerusalem with his parents to attend and participate in the Passover celebrations. At the end of the week, they were returning to Nazareth and had traveled a full day when Joseph and Mary realized Jesus was not in their traveling party. They had to turn around and return to Jerusalem to search for him."

Rebecca leaned back in her bean bag chair, crossed her arms, and shook her head. A half-smile crossed her face as she muttered, "So how do you tell God you've lost his Son?"

June smiled at the giggles erupting around the classroom.

"Good question, Rebecca. I don't know, but I'm sure Mary was doing some pretty heavy duty praying right about then. Have any of you ever been lost?"

Sheepishly, both Mandy and Lauren raised their hands, giggling as they glanced at each other, remembering the incident.

"We were only five. My mom had taken both of us shopping with her. She turned her back and was looking over some clothing racks when Lauren and I decided to do some exploring."

"We had a great time…"

"…ducking through the center of all the clothing racks…"

"…traveling up and down the different aisles…"

"Until we realized we didn't know where my mom was."

"Then it wasn't fun any more!"

"We couldn't see her anywhere…"

"…and we couldn't find our way back to where she had been!"

"It was scary!"

"We knew we were lost forever!"

They paused for breath, giving June the break she needed to jump in.

"I gather you weren't really lost forever, since you're here today!"

The other girls laughed at the exaggeration. June posed a final question to the two runaways.

"Tell me, do you remember how upset your Mom was, Mandy, when she finally found the two of you?"

Mandy and Lauren exchanged significant glances, eyes widening at the memory of the stormy response upon their rescue.

"Oh yeah!" They nodded in unison.

"So it was with Mary. Jesus appeared unconcerned. It was like he didn't know he had been lost and they had been searching for three days! Mary was upset. Can you guess why parents always react like that when they find a child they thought was lost?"

There was a pause as everyone pondered the question, trying to delve into the mysteries of the parental mind.

"Because they were scared, but now they're happy." Tina's

simple pronouncement shone with the light of truth.

"That's right! Their beloved child was lost, but now he's found!"

* * * * *

O dear God, I'm so frightened. I can't believe I lost our Son. It's the third day and still we haven't found him.

Joseph woke me before the light of dawn to continue our search. His voice sounded different this morning, almost excited in its urgency.

"Awake, Mary! We must search the temple! The thought just woke me. We haven't searched yet where he spent most of his time. The temple – we must go there next."

Joseph is excited, yet I can't believe Jesus would remain at the temple. Could he stay this long? Surely not! Even Jesus must find a place to rest.

Still, here we are hurrying in the cool darkness before dawn. Recriminations keep echoing in my mind. 'You left him! You lost him! How could you?! You left him! You lost him! How could you?' Like a refrain they're keeping time with our footsteps as we scurry over dark-cobbled roadways.

What kind of mother am I? Why didn't I check that Jesus was with our traveling party? Please, please, Father, protect him, wherever he is. Help him remain calm and not be anxious. He must know by now that we left without him. How scared he must be.

Jerusalem is such a big city and he doesn't know what it can be like. All the streets, the maze of gates and walls, the marketplace and too many areas he should stay out of. He doesn't know his way around, the places to avoid. He's so good, so pure, and there's so much evil in this world. There are many people who could hurt him.

Joseph appears calm. He keeps telling me to trust in you, Father, and I do. Yet still I can't forgive myself. I left my Son in Jerusalem alone, and only twelve years old. He may be a man in the eyes of our people, but he's still my boy.

Our frantic pace seems noisy in the quiet of a city that still sleeps, waiting for the dawn. A shiver from the cool morning brings tears to my eyes. It's so cold. Worries begin to surface. Is he warm? Is he hungry?

Give me strength, Father. I'm out of breath. Exhaustion from these last few days, rushing to and fro, covering the whole city, is wearing me down. We'd already traveled a full day's journey before realizing Jesus was not with us. Now leg muscles are screaming for rest. My stomach's churning with nausea, trying to slow me down. I can't stop. I've got to keep pushing, faster if possible. We've got to find him. If only the tears would stop, I could see my way better.

Why would Jesus do this? How could he not know it was time to leave? I know he was caught up all week in the solemnity of the Passover festival and his first visit to the temple. The priests and teachers fed his hunger for more knowledge about you, Lord. They encouraged his constant yearning to speak of you. He's always seeking the wisdom handed down through your prophets. It made sense to allow him to spend time at the feet of the most learned religious teachers of our day. He'd never had such an opportunity before. He wanted to eat, drink and sleep at the temple constantly, while the rest of us sought other activities. And yet how could he not notice the time had come for us to leave, to return to Nazareth?

Father, where do we look? Who else is left to question? No one seems to remember seeing him. Where, oh where are you, Jesus? Lord, you know all things. You know where our Son is.

Lead us to him.

The temple. Joseph keeps insisting he must be at the temple courts. I pray he is right. We must search everywhere.

The sky is growing lighter. Soon someone may be up whom we can question. Maybe one of the teachers he sat with will be there and remember him. Possibly they'll know where he has gone. Finally – I see the entrance to the temple courtyard! We're almost there.

Halting, I nearly stumble into Joseph. He's stopped suddenly, frozen in amazement ahead of me. Peering around him, I gasp at the sight before us. My heart seems to stop, catching my breath in my throat. The rising sun has sent a beam of golden light over the temple walls, focusing on the courtyard scene before us.

There he is – Jesus! Sitting amongst teachers and scholars, he's talking with them as a peer, or even a teacher. The scene is an image burned in my mind.

Learned men lean forward staring raptly into Jesus' face, eager and hungry for truth. Their eyes reflect the dawning of awe and respect, rivaling the glory of the sun's morning rays, filling the temple court. Like statues, they're holding their breath so as not to miss a word spoken from those young lips. The only movement in the morning light is Jesus gesturing as he speaks with quiet intensity. I can't hear over the pounding of my heart. Yet the teachers seem unable to move, as if Jesus' words are weaving a cord, wrapping them in the passion of his heart and soul for you, Father.

A sun ray flashes across my face, breaking the spell that gripped me. My heart is easing its pounding, but my arms and legs start to tremble, shaking with joy and relief at seeing our Son safe. Joseph supports my shoulder as I start to weave and I'm glad for his strength.

Questions burning in my mind, beg to be screamed out. 'Weren't you worried?' 'Have you been here this whole time?' 'Don't you know what we've been going through?' 'Didn't you notice the passing of hours – days, in fact!?'

Thank you, Father! You led us to our Son. But now that we've found Jesus, I just want to scream at him. Then I want to hug him. I want to weep and I want to jump for joy, but mostly I want to hold him tight. I don't want to ever lose him again.

I can see he's caught up in the world of your temple and you, Lord. He's forgotten his home, his family, even me. The man he's becoming is starting to show on his face. To be serving you, Father, is a burning desire in him.

It's too soon, Father, he's still too young. It's not safe for him to be noticed by the authorities or the public. It's not his time yet. Jesus needs to come home. I need him to come home, Father. Forgive me, but I can't keep quiet. I have to bring him back to me.

"Jesus, why have you treated us this way? Your father and I have been anxiously looking for you!"

Stopping mid-sentence, Jesus turns to gaze directly at me. I see in his expression what the teachers must have seen, dark eyes filled with a vast, world-shaping passion. Then, as if he's waking from deep thoughts, pondering the treasure of you, his heavenly Father, he returns to this mundane world.

"Why were you looking for me?" *His smile is whimsical, as though marveling that we hadn't understood sooner.* "Did you not know that I must be in my Father's house?"

What joy I sense in him! Jesus appears satisfied, like a man who has fed at a royal banquet and drunk deeply from the well of fulfillment.

Once again, Father God, I sense a wisdom and maturity so

unexpected and surprising in one so young. But he also has the courage of the young, speaking out without realizing there may be consequences of being so public. Though I know that his time has not come yet, I do not want to dampen his enthusiasm. Lord, guide us as we seek to guard Jesus and yet prepare him for his ministry calling. Jesus' desire to serve You is so overwhelming, it is hard to hold him back until the time is right.

As the years speed by, I know it will seem too soon when the time does come and he sets off to seek Your destiny for his life. O Lord, how I desire to experience the fullness of joy in You that Jesus overflows with even as he waits to fulfill his calling. Jesus will be ready; but on that day, Father God, I pray for a willing heart and a sense of peace.

My time of raising our son will soon come to an end-then into Your hands I will entrust Your Son.

Chapter Fourteen – Carpentry & Siblings

*J*une carried on with her narrative.

"After Mary and Joseph found Jesus in the temple, the Bible tells us that they returned to Nazareth and Jesus was obedient to his parents. Verse 52 in Luke chapter 2 also says, 'And Jesus increased in wisdom and in stature and in favor with God and man.'"

"What kind of statue was that?" Tina looked baffled.

June smiled at the question. Silently she applauded the other girls' tact, noticing that they had not snickered at the question. Then she wondered if they had misunderstood the word too.

"The word is 'stat-cher' not 'stat-chu'." June emphasized the difference in pronunciation. "Does anyone understand what the word 'stature' means?"

Her eyes swept across the five faces, noticing a slight shaking of heads and furrowed brows.

"Take a guess, Maria. You're good in English." June encouraged.

"Well…," Maria hesitated, "stature is something to do with your height or growth, right?"

"That's right! It can really have two meanings. The most common would be your physical growth, as in your height, like Maria said. The other definition is to do with developing in character – showing a level of greatness, in behavior or intelligence.

"So we know that Jesus continued to live in Nazareth. He went through his teen years and his twenties there. He was a young man who obeyed his parents and found favor with the adults in his hometown. He also lived a godly life because the Bible says God was pleased with him. I'm sure Jesus worked hard at his school work and with Joseph in the carpentry shop."

"I'd love to have something Jesus made in the workshop." Tina said. A sparkle lit her eyes with excitement as she exclaimed, "Don't you think Jesus would have made some beautiful pieces?"

"Like my brother," Maria sniffed. "He's always winning prizes for his woodwork projects. I couldn't cut a straight line if my life depended on it."

Rebecca suddenly sat forward, "Ms. June, didn't you say that Jesus had brothers and sisters?"

"Yes, the Bible mentions the names of four brothers and that he had sisters. The way the Scripture reads he probably had three or more sisters."

"Okay. Then what about his brothers and sisters? I know what it's like having an older sister and having all my teachers expecting me to be another Tanya!" Rebecca's eyes flashed at the burden of injustice she felt.

"That can be a tough act to follow, all right." June smiled sympathetically at Rebecca. "I see what you're getting at. Jesus must have been a tough act to follow for his younger siblings. Does anyone else ever feel that they are unfairly treated, being compared to older brothers or sisters?"

Maria nodded her head, looking at Rebecca with understanding.

While shaking their heads, Mandy and Lauren raised their hands, giggling as they answered together.

"I don't have an older sister…"

"Nor me, but my little sister is a real goodie-two-shoes…"

"Mine too, and a know-it-all."

"They both like to study and do homework!" Lauren wrinkled her nose in disgust.

"My grade five teacher even told my parents how worried she was when my sister got to her class."

"Mine too! But then she told them she was 'pleasantly surprised at the maturity of your younger daughter.'" Lauren's prim imitation of the teacher's voice brought laughter to the classroom.

June allowed the chuckles to subside. "This could bring us to another 'suppose' type of question. How do you suppose Mary would have dealt with the sibling conflicts that could have arisen?"

"With lots and lots of prayer!" Tina's answer shot out in excitement. "Isn't that what you meant by a walking prayer life?"

June couldn't help smiling as she clapped for Tina's observation.

"I'm glad you remembered. And I'm sure you must be right. Mary must have talked to God about all of her children."

* * * * *

Father, the gift Jesus carved for me is so precious. I see his love for creating beauty as a reflection of you, Lord.

Just before dinner, I was rushing with last-minute preparations, when Jesus came through the doorway and stood directly in my path, hands behind his back and that twinkle in his eyes.

"I've made you something, mother."

His voice was quiet, just for me to hear. Of course his brothers and sisters overheard his words and an immediate clamor arose. Each was trying to catch a glimpse of the treasure he was hiding.

His cheeks flushed. Amazed, I realized that Jesus was shy about giving me this gift in front of his brothers and sisters.

"It's nothing to get so excited about." He smiled at his brothers and sisters crowding around, then brought a small bowl from hiding and held it out to me.

There was a hush as we gazed in awe at the small oval shape, glistening and perfect, cradled in his roughened carpenter's hands. Gently I cupped the bowl and gazed into his face, feeling awe at the beauty of the simple gift. The small bowl seemed to glow with the fire of a craftsman who poured his heart into his trade.

In his spare time, I had watched Jesus' hands lovingly form objects out of wood, sanding and oiling the finish, bringing out the deepest beauty to be found in the piece. It was just like watching a miracle take place. He has the ability to mold the wood, almost as if he were working clay. Joseph is the only other man I know who seems able to make the wood dance and form to his will, bending it into the strongest yet most beautiful pieces.

Yet, Lord, it doesn't seem so long ago that Jesus was a small lad insisting that he help out in Joseph's shop. No task was too menial. He just loved spending time with his father. I know Joseph loved those times too.

It was almost a shame when Jesus started his schooling in the synagogue. Joseph said he missed his little helper during those hours. Yet the discussions that flourished after Jesus rushed home from school and over to the carpentry shop were more than worth the time spent apart.

Many times I'd sneak to the shop, bringing an afternoon snack and drink for their well-deserved break. Stopping just outside the doorway, I'd halt and listen to the two discussing many things. Sometimes it would be about the Scripture Jesus had studied that day. Sometimes there was a debate about the value of different woods, their strengths and hidden beauty. Eventually when I entered the shop, they'd always be working side by side, heads bent over their current task, intent on the project at hand. Contentment seems to reign whenever they're working together.

Joseph is so proud of the talent Jesus has shown. The other boys have not all taken to the craft with the same eagerness, but somehow Joseph is patiently teaching them the necessary skills to become capable carpenters.

I'm amazed at the different character traits and personalities each son has developed. Father, you've blessed Joseph and me with such wonderful children. All of them are growing up so fast into young men and women. I thank you for each of them.

It's difficult sometimes not to compare them to Jesus. I need to remind myself not to expect them to be little copies of their older brother, for it will never happen. It's so unfair to them.

Over the years, each of the younger children took turns in their hero-worship of their big brother. For years Jesus always seemed to have a little brother or sister following along, chubby legs trying to move faster to keep up with his longer stride. The piggy-back rides he gave back home, as little legs tired out, were always a reward sought by all his younger siblings.

Jesus always had so much patience and love for his little brothers and sisters. How kind he was even when they must have been an annoyance, bothering him while he read and studied his Scripture lessons.

I've lost track of how many times he's put aside his reading, or whatever he was working on, just to gather them around so he could tell stories, most often based on the Scriptures he'd been memorizing at the time.

Even the neighborhood children have clamored for his stories and attention. Sometimes our home feels like an extension of the school, especially when our yard is filled with children sitting quietly listening to Jesus.

Those early days of hero worship have long since gone. I must confess, Lord, that each of Jesus' siblings, especially his brothers, have taken turns resenting the one they can never live up to-an older brother they can never outshine. As each of our sons followed behind Jesus in school, they realized very quickly they could never fill his sandals. It was an impossible task. Unfortunately many teachers and others have expected more of them because of their brother. Father, Jesus is a hard role model to live up to and I fear the boys may give up in one way or another.

I've watched Jesus reach out to his younger brothers when they struggled with school work and patiently tutor them. Sometimes his efforts were met with resistance or a reluctance to even accept help from him, but Lord, it's amazing to watch how Jesus' love for his brothers melts down their anger or resentment. Soon they are once again laughing together, united in a close bond of brotherhood.

Lord, give me wisdom in dealing with each son and daughter as individuals. I remember once when I compared my other sons' efforts, using Jesus as a role model. I only meant to encourage them to do their best, Lord. Remind me not to do that again. I saw first-hand the hurt in their eyes. Thank you, Father, you helped me understand that I'd been unfair, causing them to feel disheartened instead.

Through you, Lord, our family has been able to heal and weather the stormy seas of emotions, especially during the years of young manhood, when passions seem to run hot. It's been difficult for them to understand that Jesus is different. I know they love their older brother so much, but they do resent being expected by others to be just like him.

Father God, give Joseph and me wisdom as we continue to encourage and teach the sons and daughters you've blessed us with. May they each learn to love and serve you, Father, each in their own way. May they be obedient to your will for their lives.

Chapter Fifteen – Joseph Gone

"Mary was pretty lucky to have Jesus as her son." Mandy nodded her head emphatically to emphasize her point.

"Why do you think that?" June queried.

Mandy started to answer, but Lauren managed to lob out the first phrase.

"Well, he was an obedient son,…"

"…and probably pretty wise,…" Mandy added.

"…and very smart."

"He was probably a great support to Mary…"

"…you know, during difficult times." Lauren triumphantly ended.

"I think you're both right," June agreed. "But I wouldn't say that Mary was lucky. I prefer to say she was blessed. Luck had nothing to do with it. God's plans were set in motion from the beginning of time. God blessed Mary when he chose her to be Jesus' mother. As such she had a large part in helping teach and raise Jesus to be the man he became."

"Of course she had help," Rebecca interjected.

"By 'help' you mean…?" June paused, waiting for someone to fill in the blanks.

"Well," holding up two fingers, Rebecca itemized her answer, "first, there was God, the heavenly Father, and second, there was Joseph, Jesus' earthly father. Both would have helped raise Jesus."

"You're right. We know God was with Mary from the beginning, helping protect and guide her while she was responsible for Jesus. Joseph was also important. Joseph would have been involved in much of the training and teaching that Jesus experienced. In a way it's too bad Joseph probably didn't live to see Jesus' ministry begin. I'm sure over the years he and Mary were looking forward to that day."

"Joseph died!?" Tina gasped the question.

A hush chilled the room as the girls looked at June, the same question written across each expression.

"We don't know when Joseph died, but it does appear that he had passed away before Jesus was thirty."

"But what about Mary?" Rebecca exclaimed. "How could she manage without a husband? They didn't have life insurance or social assistance back then."

"You're right, Rebecca. Widows depended on family or charity to help them survive. Jesus, as the oldest son, would have naturally fallen into the role of head of their household. I'm sure he kept up the carpentry shop. He must have continued training his younger brothers in the wood working trade, for he knew that carpentry was not going to be his life-long career. He may even have been involved in arranging marriages for his younger sisters, if Joseph died before they were married."

"Mary must have been so sad, though." Tina whispered quietly, a single tear balancing at the corner of her eye. "I wonder how Jesus felt at the death of his Dad, well, I mean his earthly father?"

June quietly passed a tissue to Tina. "I would imagine Jesus grieved deeply for Joseph. But he also knew, without a doubt, there would be a heavenly reunion. I would suppose Mary felt blessed even at this time in her life. She had Jesus, not only to help take care of the family, but also to comfort her in her loss."

* * * * *

How long has it been, Father God? How long since I slept through the night, on a pillow not soaked by my tears? I can hardly believe this new day has begun with such hope blossoming in my heart. Thank you, Lord, for you've answered the prayer of Jesus, our loving Son.

Was it only yesterday I woke up crying out to you? I felt numb and wanted to keep it that way. The hurt was buried deep, cutting into my heart and soul. I think everyone was fooled by the busyness I kept hiding behind. Everyone that is, except Jesus. I could see it in his gaze when he looked at me. The look of sorrow and concern shining from his eyes nearly melted the wall of ice I was keeping around my emotions. I was afraid to look directly at him because I knew he'd reach inside and melt the barrier I was desperate to keep. I feared the pain. It would hurt too much to lose that wall of numbness.

Lord, I've felt frozen since the day Joseph died. Until last night I was sure I'd never feel anything again, nor did I want to. It just hurt too much. Over these last few weeks-or has it been months?- I've tried talking to you, Father. I never found the words. Only sobs and tears came out. I still can't believe he's gone.

Oh, my beloved Joseph. How can I carry on without your quiet wisdom and strength? You carried this family on your strong shoulders as easily as you would bring a small sapling slung across your back to your carpentry shop. Closing my eyes, I can still see you across the field searching for wood, carrying huge loads, with little Jesus following behind. Even when he could barely walk, Jesus would insist on helping. You'd load him up with small sticks, praising him for carrying his own small load.

I miss looking into your eyes, Joseph. So many seasons of life shone from your gaze. How many times I remember laughter sparkling in your eyes as your zest for living burst forth. How often have I shared the sacred joy burning in your gaze as we worshipped our God. But most of all I miss that special look of love you saved only for me.

Throughout the day, I still catch myself straining to hear the deep timbre of your voice. The workshop seems quiet without the joyful abandon of your laughter. It was such a pleasure to hear you and Jesus laughing in your workshop and, though I couldn't hear the joke, I'd smile, knowing that you two were enjoying the fellowship of being together as father and son.

You loved Jesus so much and were a good father to him. It seemed effortless the way you accepted who he is and embraced him as a son. I'm not sure I ever said how proud of you I was, how you dealt with Jesus as a child, and then as a young man, teaching him with a God-given wisdom and respect.

It was an honor to watch the two of you working side by side, conversing about the Lord and all the mysteries of life. I was always grateful you were there to answer the never-ending queries. All of those how-and why-questions baffled me and yet you took joy in helping train his young mind. Your life was a living example of a deep faith and love for our heavenly Father. We had dreamed of watching together the mystery of Jesus' kingdom unfold. One more dream left unfulfilled.

Lord, you took my dear Joseph much too soon. Still I trust in you and your wisdom.

These weeks have dragged by in a fog. I can hardly remember what's happened. Each day blended into another, all the same, all alike, all colorless.

One memory does stand out clearly in my mind. I remember vividly the look on Jesus' face the day we said goodbye to Joseph. The sparkle of life and joy in Jesus' eyes was for that moment quenched with tears of grief. The depth of sorrow he felt overwhelmed me, even through my own grief. Together we stood, a family feeling broken, arms around each other, weeping for the one we loved and had lost.

I'd never seen Jesus grieve that deeply at death before. He always seemed able to see past the end of it to something far better. He often spoke of a new life, a new beginning. And yet this time I could see him sorrowing for the physical absence of the earthly father he loved deeply.

Dear Father, I realize how much our Son has helped me during these weeks. I've depended on him, maybe too much. Help me to be there again for my family, not only for Jesus but also for the other children. They may be grown, or almost, yet they grieve at the absence of their father too.

Last evening I finally woke from this sleep that had overtaken me. Until then I was carrying on with daily chores, cooking and cleaning, but inside I felt hollow. My love for Joseph was burning a hole in my soul and I didn't know how to heal it. I've missed him terribly.

Nighttime is always the worst. Trying to sleep alone in the bed where we shared a short lifetime of love and joyous communion, is lonely. I'm not sure if Jesus and the others heard my muffled sobs night after night, but I know you heard, Father, and understood my anguished cries for help. Lord, thank you for starting to heal my grieving spirit, for giving me a song in my heart once again.

What a change you brought about since last evening.

Yesterday had been the usual fog-filled day. After supper I rushed around cleaning dishes and leftovers from the table. Afraid to stop, afraid to sit still, I kept busy. I knew feelings would begin to well up as soon as I quit my hectic pace and I had to be strong for my family.

Finally Jesus stopped me, wrapping his strong arms around me to quiet my activity and gain my attention. He looked into my face, his smile gentle, his eyes filled with compassion and a knowing grief of his own.

I closed my eyes, nearly panicking at the thought, "He knows! I can't look into his eyes or the pain will overcome me!"

"Leave it for now, Mother. The others will finish. Come with me."

Without question I let him lead me outside, up the hill to "his tree". I knew that was where we were going, because he always went there. Mostly alone, early in the morning he would slip out of the house and spend time alone with you, Father.

As he was leading me up the path, I remembered many other mornings when he'd wake Joseph and the two of them would grab a handful of the smoked fish I kept in the earthen jar for a morning snack. Together they would disappear to "his tree". Occasionally I felt a twinge of jealousy as I watched them return, always with joy in their eyes and a spring in their step. I could see your heavenly reflection in their faces on those mornings, Lord.

Now it was my turn.

Carefully Jesus was guiding me up the dark pathway, an arm steadying me as my tired feet tripped on the unfamiliar darkness of the path. His own steps had worn a trail and he knew the way blindly. I felt like an old woman, needing support climbing such a short distance. Indeed I knew I had aged a lot in a short time. Bruised eyes, empty and hopeless, would stare back at me, reflected in the water each morning. I couldn't bear to look at this old woman, for I didn't want to see what I was becoming.

Placing a soft blanket against the base of his favorite tree, Jesus gently helped me sit on the cushioned ground. He joined me and we sat quietly for some time. I supposed Jesus was enjoying the nighttime sounds, feeling pleasure in the soft breeze refreshing our skin after a hot day. I, however, could only hear my heart throbbing, and feel tears threatening to spill over. I swallowed back painful sobs, trying to keep them prisoner lest they break out, destroying the peaceful moment.

Jesus' arm circled behind me, cushioning my back against the hard tree trunk. With a soft squeeze of compassion, he finally broke the quiet that surrounded us.

"We'll be together with him again one day. I promise."

They were simple words, softly spoken. It was his promise. Suddenly a glimmer of hope started to glow in my mind, its rays burning through the fog, warming my soul, finally reaching my heart buried behind its wall of frozen emotions. Turning to him, I poured my grief into his arms. He wept with me. As tears subsided, I could hear Jesus' whispered prayer to you, Lord.

"Give Mother both rest and peace, Father. Comfort her through the pain of grief. Help sorrow turn to joy. May she relish memories of a deep love, but live in the hope and knowledge of a heavenly reunion. Return to her the joy of you and your gifts of life, love, family and friends."

Dear Father, how I thank you for the gift of our Son and his love for me. As Jesus spoke those words, I felt your comfort wash over me, cleansing and healing. I know you answered his prayer, for when I came down from that place a burden had lifted and my *step was that of a much younger woman again.*

I still miss my beloved Joseph and I always will. But I also know one day we will be reunited. Give him my love, Father, and tell him I'll see him later.

Chapter Sixteen – Cousin John

"Mary had the blessing of Jesus living at home in Nazareth until he was thirty years old." As June continued her narrative she was quickly interrupted.

"Thirty! Isn't that kind of old to still live with your Mom?" Lauren exclaimed.

"By today's standards, it may seem so," June smiled at the question. "Don't forget that as head of the family now, Jesus was responsible for supporting Mary and any of his younger brothers or sisters who were living at home. But one day when Jesus was thirty years old, everything changed.

"News reached Nazareth that a prophet was baptizing people, calling for repentance, preparing for the kingdom of heaven. Can you guess who that prophet was?"

"It was John the Baptist, of course." Maria declared with her usual confidence.

"You're right, Maria," June smiled her thanks at the answer. "Cousin John had come in from the desert where he had been living and was now beginning his ministry. In the Old Testament, there was a prophecy that the forerunner of the Messiah would come as 'A voice of one calling in the desert, "Prepare the way of the Lord, make straight paths for him".' This prophecy was fulfilled in John.

As had been promised to Elizabeth and Zechariah, John was the prophet that would prepare the way for God's Messiah."

"So, if John was preparing the way," Rebecca paused a moment, then continued, "well, when Jesus heard the news he must have known that it was time for him to start his ministry, right?"

"Yes, Rebecca, the time had come. Jesus traveled from Nazareth, south towards the Jordan River and he was baptized by John. Does anyone remember what happened immediately after he was baptized?" June looked expectantly around the circle of girls.

Mandy raised her hand while answering the question simultaneously. "God spoke when Jesus rose up from the water and said, 'You are my beloved Son; with you I am well pleased'. Well, it was something along that line."

"Very good, Mandy!" June beamed at the young woman. She was always being surprised at what these girls hid under all their giggling. "So where did Jesus go immediately after his baptism?"

Not to be outdone, Lauren jumped in to take up the question. "Jesus went into the wilderness for forty days where he prayed and fasted and was tempted by the devil."

"Correct, Lauren!" June gave her thumbs up.

"Ms. June," Tina timidly raised her hand to catch June's attention. "What about Mary? Did she know that it was time for Jesus' ministry to start? I mean, this meant he was leaving home for good, right?"

"Thank you, Tina, for bringing up a good question and reminding us that our lesson today is mainly about Mary. I think this is another 'suppose' type question. We can't read in the Bible what Mary's response was when Jesus left to see Cousin John. I can only suppose that Mary was probably torn between emotions. In one way she'd rejoice that Jesus' ministry was beginning, but she also faced what all parents do when their son or daughter leaves home. I'm sure it was a difficult farewell for Mary."

"You mean the 'empty nest syndrome'," Tina added while nodding agreement at June's summary. "I think it would have been very difficult for Mary. A child leaving home is pretty much the end of a parent's job, right? So in a way, Mary might have felt her work was done."

"Well put, Tina, well put."

*   *   *   *   *

Father God, is it true? The stories of the one called 'The Baptizer' have reached our ears. He is preaching and baptizing the people. They say he is calling for repentance because the kingdom of God is near.

Could it be John?

It's been so long since we've heard about John and now the people are telling of a prophet emerging from the desert. They say this man wears woven camel hair clothing, his hair has never been shorn, as a Nazirite, and he lives on a diet of wild honey and locusts. It's difficult to equate this picture with the young man we last saw years ago. Elizabeth and Zechariah raised John in the Nazirite traditions as instructed by the angel before his birth, separate and dedicated to the Lord. After they passed away, John seemed to disappear completely into the desert wilderness.

When Jesus heard the news about the new baptizing prophet, he looked over at me. I saw in his eyes the certainty that this was indeed the moment he had been waiting for.

"I need to go see John, mother."

As I bowed my head, his arms gently hugged me. He knew I

was trying to keep all my fears in check.

"Are you so sure that it's your cousin, Jesus? Maybe you should wait a little longer."

I couldn't help the hopeful note in my voice, even though in my heart I knew Jesus was right. Since the day we lost him in Jerusalem when he was twelve, I've discouraged him from becoming too public in his zeal for you, Lord.

"It's not your time yet" became a refrain I repeated over and over. For years I've feared the reaction of those in power. After saving our baby from Herod's wrath I've always felt the need to be careful about attracting attention from those in authority. Lord, you know I've prayed many times over the years that we would know when it was his time.

Last night we sat together, not talking, just being together. He was leaving in the morning and I didn't want to miss a moment of time with him. It was very late and I realized I was being selfish. Jesus needed his strength for the journey. Finally I arose and brought out the special garment I had been working on for a long time. It was the seamless tunic I had spent hours pouring my love into. Though the weaving was difficult, it was such a simple-looking garment. I want him to wear it close to his heart, Lord. Then I will feel a part of me will be with him wherever he is.

"For you, my son," was all I could manage to whisper as I placed the garment in his lap.

I could tell he was pleased even though my tears had drawn a hazy curtain across his expression. The love in his eyes still managed to shine through.

The morning came too soon. Saying goodbye was even more difficult than I'd imagined, Father. He set off down the road and disappeared through a blur of tears. I had clung to him as he said *farewell and I know I made it difficult for him to leave. Somehow I feel I let him down by not showing excitement about the prospect of his ministry. I'm sure Joseph would have been much stronger than I was while saying goodbye.*

The only sorrow I saw in his eyes was when he realized his brothers wouldn't even say "goodbye". They made sure they were extra early at the workshop this morning, so they wouldn't have to watch him leave. They don't understand at all. To them Jesus has just abandoned us and a decent lifestyle to go and do something "crazy". Yet none of their comments, or my own hesitancy fazed Jesus as he took to the road this morning.

Jesus is facing the future with such assurance. Why was I so hesitant to see this day come to pass? It's been a long time arriving. You blessed me with his presence at home for so much longer than I'd hoped for and yet I'm still hesitant. I realize our life is changing; it has taken another direction.

I'm proud of the way Jesus has been the head of our household since Joseph died. Over the years he has prepared his younger brothers well. I know they're capable of taking over the carpentry business. Jesus was diligent in running the shop, building it so that it was able to support us. It seemed to be a labor of love for him. Not just the love of working with wood, but also as a tribute to Joseph.

Lord, I'm also grateful for Jesus' wisdom as he helped me arrange marriages for his sisters. Each seems satisfied and happy with their husbands, all godly men. It is difficult knowing that none of his brothers or sisters agree with his decision to leave, nor do they understand who Jesus is. Yet I know they are each beloved to Jesus, and he is satisfied that they are all settled, able to carry on their lives without him.

Why do I feel I'm the only one not prepared for this day?

Father, I'm filled with a mixture of emotions. In one way I rejoice at the joy in Jesus' eyes as he eagerly begins your work. Yet I mourn the loss of our quiet life together.

I've treasured our times of close communion and even the silly jokes and playful moments we shared. So many precious memories accompany me as I wander around our empty home. Echoes of laughter, the hum of songs, murmured prayers, the whisper of voices sharing long into the night, are all that keep me company in the quiet house.

Jesus has disappeared down the pathway, out of sight, on his way to a destiny I've never fully understood. It's at times like this that I miss Joseph the most. He'd be the strong one, able to support and applaud Jesus' incredible desire to please you. I do too, Lord, but not yet with the enthusiasm I should feel. I don't have Joseph at my side to help me face the emptiness of the house behind me. As always, it's you, Lord, whom I depend upon. In my own strength I can't seem to feel anything past the ache in my heart. Help me, Father God. Give me peace and courage as our Son walks a new pathway.

Please, Father, be with Jesus. Keep him safe. Help me know how I can support and encourage him when he comes home, even if only for a short while. Let me truly rejoice and praise him for his dedication to you.

Lord, I am still your handmaiden and seek to know what you would have me do now. Has my work in the life of our Son ended? It's difficult to understand the role I'll have in Jesus' life, if any.

Father, I know I'll always be his mother. I guess a mother's love is the one treasure I'll always be able to give him.

Chapter Seventeen – A Wedding in Cana

*J*ne turned in her Bible to the gospel of John. Looking up at the circle of girls, she glanced at the clock and was startled that the time had flown by so quickly.

"We've come to the end of our lesson, just as Mary had come to the end of her private family life with Jesus."

As a sigh of disappointment whispered through the group, June appreciated the contradiction, remembering their groans at the beginning of the class. They'd really become involved with the lesson today, June realized, and felt a sense of accomplishment.

"I'd like to end with one more encounter between Mary and Jesus that was recorded for us in the gospel of John.

"The event was a wedding in the town of Cana. Mary and Jesus were both there. Jesus' ministry had just begun. He had started choosing some of his disciples but had not called all of them yet. The wine had run out by the third day of the celebrations. This was considered a disaster for the family hosting the wedding.

"Mary called Jesus over and told him about the need. Up to this time Jesus had not performed any public miracles. Jesus' response to Mary seems unusual and unexpected. In chapter two, verse four, Jesus said to Mary, 'Woman, what does this have to do with me? My hour has not yet come.' Does anyone else find that an unusual response?"

Several heads nodded in agreement as Rebecca burst out, "First of all, why would he call her 'Woman'? She's his Mom, for goodness sake! And secondly, why did he say his time had not come yet?"

"Yeah," Maria took up the challenge, "didn't we just decide he knew it was time when John the Baptist started his ministry?"

"Calm down, ladies." June held up her hand to quiet the disgruntled muttering. "I'm sure Jesus was not being disrespectful addressing his mother as 'Woman'. He may have been making a point. Maybe it was to help Mary understand that she was not just his mother. Mary, like all people, needed to see Jesus as her Savior and Messiah, not just as her Son anymore."

"What did Mary say back to Jesus?" Tina asked.

"Mary simply instructed the servants to do whatever Jesus told them to do. Jesus went ahead and performed his first public miracle, changing water into wine."

Lauren's brow wrinkled in confusion as she asked, "So why did Jesus say to Mary that it wasn't his time and then go ahead and do a miracle?"

"Does anyone have any ideas why Jesus might have said that to Mary?" June asked, watching the girls struggle with the problem.

"Maybe Jesus was waiting for his mother to give him permission to, well you know, go public?" Mandy dislodged some of her pillow nest as she sat up to explain, "You know, sort of giving him her permission, or blessing, to show people his heavenly power?"

June smiled at the young faces surrounding her. They really are wonderful girls, so full of eagerness. What a blessing this class is to me, she realized.

"That's a very insightful thought, Mandy. No one can say whether you're right or wrong. In fact, the only one who can answer that question would be Jesus or Mary herself."

*   *   *   *   *

Father God, I feel like I gave my Son away today. Though it wasn't his wedding, somehow I know, just like the groom, he's left my home and no longer belongs to my family. Now he belongs to the world.

It was a beautiful wedding. The bride and groom looked so young, so hopeful, yet so scared. It brought back many memories of Joseph and me at the beginning of our married life. How I miss him! He would've been proud of your Son today. Jesus was amazing.

The wedding celebrations had carried on for three days. As usual everyone seemed reluctant to see an end to the joyous occasion. When I saw shame and horror on the hostess' face, I sought her out to see what the problem was.

Father, her face crumpled and through tears she whispered that the wine had run out. I knew their meager savings had already been stretched just to serve what they had at the wedding banquet. As tears continued to roll down her cheeks, she moaned at the humiliation they would suffer. This could ruin what she hoped would be the greatest time of the young couple's life. My heart melted at her tears and I knew something had to be done to save the starry-eyed bride and groom from an embarrassing disaster.

Lord, as I pulled Jesus away from his followers, he looked like he knew what I was going to ask of him, but didn't want to be pushed. Still I remembered the mother's tears and pled with Jesus to do something.

"They have no wine."

It was a simple statement, Lord. I knew Jesus grasped my meaning. He's your Son so I knew he could solve their problem. But his reply spoke of a reluctance to begin a public show of power before he felt ready to begin his new life.

"Woman, what does this have to do with me? My hour has not yet come."

As he called me "woman," I suddenly saw Jesus as a man who is more than just my Son. He is a man, but more importantly, Father, he's your Son, the Son of God. He's grown from the baby I loved, protected and cherished. Now he's ready and willing to become my Savior as well as the Messiah of the people.

Such simple words, "My hour has not yet come." I wondered at his hesitation. Did he doubt his readiness? In my mother's heart I knew he was ready. I knew his time had come.

He had shared with me the wonder of your words at his baptism by John, "You are My beloved Son; with you I am well pleased." He had also shared with me the trials and temptations he'd faced and overcame in the desert. He was ready.

Then I wondered if he knew it was I who wasn't ready. Was he remembering how reluctant I was to see him go? Lord, I know he was born for a special purpose. What your plan for him is I've never completely understood. But it has begun whether I am ready or not.

The noise of wedding guests faded into a muffled background. I felt deaf and blind to my surroundings. I only saw Jesus' love as I stared deeply into his eyes. Like a lightning bolt, it struck me that just as parents of a bride or groom give their child away, so now it was my turn. Father, you sent your Son into this world. Now I, his mother, had to release him to the people, for that's where he's needed.

Just as a wedding means a new beginning so it also means an ending. In the same way, Lord, I see Jesus leaving his family to begin a new life of ministry for you. In my heart I wanted to tell him I understood. His ministry was beginning and I too was ready at last. He'd honored Joseph, by the years he provided for the needs of our family. Now it was time to begin his heavenly Father's work. I realized Jesus was waiting for my blessing.

Jesus received your heavenly blessing as he rose from his baptismal waters. Now it was my turn. After years of waiting, assuring him that it wasn't his time yet, I could now affirm that his time had come. He could reveal himself to the world. I was willing to see him go.

Looking deep into his eyes, I smiled and nodded in understanding. In that look I shared my love and my blessing, from the depth of my heart.

I called a couple of servants over and instructed them.

"Do whatever he tells you."

That is my prayer for the world, Lord. That they will hear Jesus' words and do 'whatever he tells you.'

He understood, Father. Jesus simply commanded the servants to fill the stone jars with water and take a cup to the Master of the banquet. As the servants obeyed, it was no longer water, but the most glorious wine ever tasted! Many people never even realized the miraculous nature of that wine, but I knew.

As great as that miracle was, to me there is a greater miracle happening. Jesus is beginning to allow the world to see who he truly is. He is revealing himself, becoming vulnerable, and placing himself in the hands of a sinful, fallen world.

I admit, Father, that I fear turning Jesus over to the people. Will they love and care for him as much as I do? Will they see the depth of his love and his gentle kindness? Will they accept his purity, the beauty of his soul? Or will they despise him, reject him? I've been filled with so many fears facing this day that I knew was coming.

As always, Lord, I rest in you. I place Jesus fully into your care. Take him and strengthen him. Guide him as he walks this new pathway. I know he's never alone, for you are there, just as you always have been. Just as in my heart I'll always be with him too.

* * * * *

"Each of you has brought up some interesting ideas today. I'm going to leave them with you." June quietly closed her Bible as she smiled at her attentive audience. "Try to remember the Bible is made up of real people, experiencing real life. What one thing will you take home with you today from the life of Mary?"

Each girl volunteered an idea.

"Mary was a godly woman, which doesn't mean perfect."

"Mary loved God and was obedient to him."

"Mary faced some pretty scary things, but God was always with her, helping her."

"Mary must have had a strong prayer life…"

"…A walking prayer life!" Tina finished off triumphantly.

June clapped her hands at the enthusiastic answers.

"That's an impressive list. These are all good qualities and lessons for each of us to remember. A lot has happened in Mary's life even though we've stopped right at the beginning of Jesus' ministry.

"For the next three years, Mary watched her son carry out his ministry. She was with him during some of his travels. We know Mary was at the cross when Jesus died and was at the tomb three days later to hear of his resurrection. Can you imagine the joy she felt knowing Jesus had accomplished the will of his heavenly Father? She watched

Jesus' ascension into heaven and heard his promise that he would prepare a place for us.

"The last time Jesus and Mary spoke happened as he was dying on the cross. Jesus made sure his mother would be cared for. He gave the responsibility to John, also known as the 'beloved disciple.' What a caring son."

"Ms. June, do you suppose..." Tina's question came to a stammering a halt.

"Another 'suppose' question?" June chuckled with all the girls. "Okay, let's hear your question, Tina."

"Well it's not really a suppose question. What I really wanted to know is, do you think we'll get a chance to ask all of these 'suppose' questions to Mary when we get to heaven?"

June's eyes swept the group of young faces. Each one was so fresh and eager for life, always seeking answers, always willing to learn.

Sudden tears glistened in her eyes as she silently prayed. *Thank you, Lord, for answering my earlier question. I know why I agreed to teach these girls. You love them so much and I believe I do too!*

"I'm sure she'll be happy to answer all of your questions, Tina. All of them."

The girls began filing out of the classroom, tripping and giggling through the doorway. Quiet began to descend upon the room once more. June smiled as she hummed to herself, picking up the empty plate, scattered papers, piling beanbags in the corner. Once more she worked around the room, closing windows, sweeping crumbs and completing the finishing touches to put the class to rest for another week. The lights flickered off, calm tucked in as the room settled back to sleep.

June sighed, her heart overflowing with emotion from the session. It was a joy watching these young women as they grew spiritually.

Lord Jesus, your mother was an incredible woman. Like Tina, I also hope to talk with Mary. What a life she lived! What wonderful stories she must have to tell!

After one final glance around the room, she shut the door. Her footsteps echoed down the hall, as Ms. June began planning for next week's class.

Epilogue

The woman sat in a chair overlooking the garden outside her window. Her face was lined with years of life. So many joys and sorrows had left their indelible mark, yet the gentle sweet spirit continued to radiate. Vestiges of the young woman shone through. But now a greater joy and peace shone forth, born of the knowledge that her life had been good.

Her voice, still shaky but pure, was lifted in a song of praise.

"Be exalted, O God, above the heavens!
Let Your glory be over all the earth!"

She gasped for breath. Singing was a pleasure she would forego for now, she decided. There had been many joys in her life. Many tears as well, but the Lord had truly blessed her.

A tear slipped down the crease of her cheek as she sat remembering some of the miraculous events she had lived through. It was unbelievable what God had allowed her to experience in her lifetime.

The young girl she once was had held a simple dream-to honor God by living in obedience to him. She had thought this would mean living a simple, quiet life, being a faithful wife, raise children and teach them to follow God. A small smile touched her lips at the memory of those innocent dreams. The deep lines in her face were molded by a woman who had truly loved life and laughed with joy many times over the years.

"I do miss my dear Joseph. I only wish we had been able to share these years together."

Her audible whisper was a habit she had taken to recently. Speaking her inner thoughts out loud seemed to comfort her in these twilight years. She was missing the companionship of many loved ones as they slowly disappeared over the years.

The door to her room opened, and a swarthy face looked in at the beloved woman sitting comfortably.

"Did you say something, Mother?"

Mary opened her eyes and beamed a welcoming smile at the man gazing at her with concern in his eyes.

Dear John! No wonder he was your beloved disciple, Jesus. He's been a blessing to me since you left us. Just as you asked him, he has taken care of me as though I were truly his mother. Even in your agony, your thoughts were always for others. How you loved all of us!

"Yes, dear John, I did speak. But it's only the ramblings of an old woman living with her memories."

Her answer did not alleviate the frown on his forehead. Searching her face for signs of ailing, he finally gave a whimsical smile in return.

"You have many memories to keep you company! Do you need anything? Are you warm enough? Can I get you a drink of water?"

"Don't worry so, John. I'm content just sitting here. You take such good care of me. Our Savior could not have asked for a better son to watch over and care for me."

He flushed at the compliment and shook his head.

"It's my honor and privilege. I couldn't have asked for a more enjoyable task. Your early memories of Jesus have blessed me over the years. Rest now, mother. You're looking more tired these days."

Slowly he closed the door on Mary's privacy, wondering what could be weakening her normally strong constitution. He had noticed a definite lessening in her usual energy. Though looking more fragile, a glowing peace seemed to be shining from her weakening gaze these days.

Mary closed her eyes as the effort of carrying on a conversation had drained what little strength she seemed to have.

Drifting into a semi-sleep her mind began to replay some of the highlights of her life. Faces crossed her memory, drifting through the passages of time. Early years with her parents and sister, followed by cousin Elizabeth and Zechariah, then beloved Joseph. The wonder of a sweet newborn Jesus, rough-cut shepherds with faces awash with awe and wonder, the foreign magi bowing low to worship at the feet of a toddler.

Like leaves tumbling in the wind, her memories of the years swirled past quickly. More recent faces swept through her mind, a band of simple men chosen by Jesus. Then she was overwhelmed by the expressions on crowds of faces, those experiencing the power of God in their lives, healing, broken lives mended, hope reborn in the hopeless. Memories of miracles piled high, knocking into one another-water into wine, feeding the multitude, healing the lame, the blind, the demon-possessed, raising the dead.

God was there, plain to anyone who would use their eyes of faith. No one could have seen what she had seen and not know that Jesus was the Son of God. He was all he claimed to be and at the foot of his cross she finally understood Simeon's words.

Watching her son die was a sword that had cut deep into her heart and soul. She knew this was where God had been leading Jesus and was thankful that she hadn't understood completely from the beginning.

"I don't know if I'd have been brave enough to say yes to you, Father God," she murmured, a tear slowly trailing down the lines carved at the side of her eyes.

The memory of those dark hours around Golgotha always brought tears. This was her Son – the baby so miraculously conceived, so wonderfully announced, so well-protected, and loved. He was the pride and joy of her mother's heart. Watching him die was a horror that she could not turn from, but how she wanted to hide from seeing him hung tortured, bleeding and dying.

"I wanted to hold you in my arms and wipe the blood from your face," she whispered. "I needed to look into your beautiful eyes and see the love I always found there. I wanted to make it all right. But I couldn't. No one could. Only you could, Jesus. You had the power but you had made your choice. You were obedient right to the end."

As the dark memory faded it was replaced by the sweet joy of the resurrection morning! A smile lit her face as once again she relived the moment when she first laid eyes on her resurrected Son. No, she corrected herself, my resurrected Lord and Savior. How magnificent he looked! He was the same beloved Jesus, yet in some way more regal. He had finished his work here, opening the doorway to heaven for all of us.

"Even after all these years, I still feel unworthy to have been chosen, to be included in your plans, Lord," she whispered.

A bright light seemed to fill the chamber and Mary opened her tired eyes. Was it a vision of an angel, she wondered? But no, as the figure drew closer her weak eyes seemed to suddenly clear. Nail-pierced hands were held out to her. Recognition was immediate and without fear, she eagerly reached her aged trembling hands toward the One who was there to escort her home.

"Come, Mother. Father God says it's time. Come home to your reward. You've been a good and faithful servant. As I promised years ago, there's someone else anxiously awaiting your arrival!"

Her hands were grasped in Jesus' strong grip. She could feel the freedom of new life flow through her soul. In the distance her eyes could make out the smiling face of her beloved Joseph, gesturing her to come, hastening her journey to the heavenly side.

Joy burst like a rocket as she felt herself drawn upward, ever nearer to the Presence she had always tried to draw close to in life. Now there was more love than she had ever dreamed possible. She could feel him everywhere!

"Yes, Father God. It's me…Mary. I'm coming home!"

CPSIA information can be obtained at www.ICGtesting.com
Printed in the USA
LVOW042104160812

294507LV00002B/9/P